HER SHIFTER MATES

PERFECT PAIRS BOOK 5

TAMSIN BAKER

AMELIA SHAW

ONE

NANCY.

A strange thump followed by a loud crack made the bike swerve and jump. The grinding of gears in my beloved bike's engine confirmed my worst fears.

"Oh no, baby, no." Damn it! I'd been so careful. I'd gotten all this way without a scratch.

I looked back but couldn't see anything in the road. Whatever it was must have run off into the woods lining the side of the road.

I eased off the accelerator and let the bike coast as I passed a sign like many others I'd seen on this trip. I'd just entered another town of less than ten thousand people. The last thing I wanted was to get stuck in a place like that.

The bike began to jolt and the engine protested more loudly. Ah crap. "Hold on, baby."

The scenery began to change. The miles of road and empty lots became pretty houses and then a strip of shops. I slowed right down, looking for signs of a bike shop, or a mechanic. Anyone who might be able to help with my current predicament.

A strange shiver coursed over my body, making the hairs on my arms stand up. What the hell was that? I glanced around. Was there danger nearby? What was I sensing?

I pulled over and pushed up the visor on my helmet as a woman pushing a large black pram drew abreast of me. "Excuse me," I called out to her and she stopped, assessed me, then walked closer.

"Yes?"

"My bike needs a mechanic. Are there any good ones around here?"

The girl smiled. "Actually, yeah. Toni's the best at bikes."

"Great." I hoped to hell that Tony wasn't a dick. "Where's the shop?"

"Down that street." The girl pointed. "Big red sign. You can't miss it."

"Thanks heaps," I said, snapping shut my visor and carefully riding my motorbike the final half block to our new destination.

I should count myself lucky to have made it this far without crashing, or breaking down. But I was only two days away from reaching safety. Surely, this Tony would be able to fix my bike enough so that we could limp through the final leg of our escape?

The closer I got to the workshop, the more unlikely my fast getaway became. The sound of crunching gears was growing louder and my stomach twisted with a mix of worry and hunger. I hadn't eaten in too long, having chosen not to stop for breakfast, or dinner last night.

I saw the sign that I was told I wouldn't miss, and the chick was right. The sign was red and neon and someone had painted an amazing bike in graffiti-style artwork on the bricks beside the garage.

My sorta place.

A woman in jeans and a gray tank walked out the open garage door and waved me into a parking spot behind the shop.

She probably heard me coming a mile off.

I pulled my Harley into the spot she indicated and lifted off my helmet with a tug.

This was going to be expensive. I could already tell.

"How can I help you?" the woman asked, crossing her arms over her chest and studying me with interest.

I didn't turn the engine off because I knew she'd probably want to listen to it. Instead, I kicked out the bike stand and swung my leg over the seat to dismount. "I hope you can. I hit something just outside your town. I think it was some sort of small squirrel, or something. Now my bike's not running right."

It could have been a fox, or a cat. I honestly had no idea. I'd been lost in my own head when it happened and it had been so quick.

The woman, who had long brown hair, squatted down next to my beast of a machine. "Sounds like the carbie's stuffed."

I groaned, pulling off my gloves and unzipping my leather jacket. I was hot and sweaty, and now I was also pissed. Not a great combination. "Yeah, I know. Fuck it. Just my luck."

I turned off the bike and pocketed the keys. No point leaving it running now.

The girl held out her hand and smiled like she had to deal with people breaking down outside her shop all the time. "I'm Lexie."

"Nancy," I said, shaking her offered hand and then shrugging out of the heavy jacket. "I need to be on the road again as soon as possible. When can you fix this up, do you think?"

This wasn't good. In fact, the situation could turn into a royal mess. I'd gotten away smoothly and probably had a few days' head start on the guys chasing me, but that didn't mean I'd stay ahead now.

Lexie grimaced, glancing inside the shop. "I can't give you a time, but you're in the best place for a bike like this. Come in for a drink, meet Toni the owner, and she can give you an idea of when she can squeeze you in."

"She?" I smiled, pleasantly surprised. "This is an all-girl mechanic shop?" Exactly the sort I would have run if I could have.

She laughed. "Don't think that was Toni's intention... exactly. But she runs everything, and I just came on. So... yeah."

I managed to take my first deep breath in what felt like forever. "It's all good," I said, more than a little relieved to not be dealing with some overweight know-it-all man. "I just… didn't expect it, I guess."

Female mechanics were rare enough. But one that knew bikes and owned her own shop? That was a rare combination.

"Come on in." Lexie gestured for me to follow her. "You look like you could use a coffee. Or something even stronger."

I chuckled. "Something stronger. Definitely."

I followed Lexie through the garage workshop area and into the office, stepping around another woman who hopped up from under a bike and gave me a quick look before heading outside.

I stared after her but didn't say anything as she disappeared from my sight. I assumed she was probably the Toni in question, and wondered if she'd gone to have a look at my Harley.

Lexie offered me a coffee with a shot of whiskey which I accepted gratefully, before glancing around the old-school office. "This looks like a great place to work."

Lexie grinned. "Yeah, it's not modern or anything, but it kinda feels like home, doesn't it?"

"It does."

The other woman walked back into the office then, wiping her hands on an oil rag.

Lexie gestured to her. "Nancy, this is Toni."

Toni didn't bother with introductions. "Your transmission's shot, and the carbie's got a hole in it the size of my fist."

I covered my face with my hands. "Oh no." That was the worst news I'd heard in days. How the hell was I going to pay for that? And how long would it take to fix?

"I can fix it for you," the mechanic went on. "Around the jobs I've already got booked in, but the main problem is that transmission."

I took some steadying breaths and dropped my hands away from my face. I had some money in my savings account I could dig into, but if it wasn't enough, what was I going to do?

I faced the woman who held my fate in her hands, though she didn't know it yet. "You don't have another one, do you?"

"Another transmission?" Toni clarified, before shrugging. "It's a custom part. I can order it in, but it'll take a week."

I gulped. "And money." But the question was, how much.

"Yep." She named a figure that made me gulp. "That's only an estimate but it'll be in that ballpark. And I'll need the money upfront for the part, I'm afraid."

I stifled my groan. Of course, she did. I didn't blame her; she had a business to run, after all.

"And it's completely unrideable?" I asked, hoping for a miracle somehow.

The mechanic nodded. "If you'd traveled any further, you'd probably have blown the engine completely."

Then the bike would be useless and I may as well leave it here and try to hitch a ride over the state line.

Stop being melodramatic and face facts.

I stood up and started pacing the room, running over the numbers in my bank account and allowing for gas and a little food. "Okay... okay. I can cover the cost of the parts. But I've got nowhere to stay while I'm here. I won't have anything spare for... err..."

Living.

Maybe they knew someone with a couch I could crash on?

I wasn't sure I could pay for the labor yet, either, but I'd get a job doing something here. Surely, after everything I'd done to get away from my old life, a little squirrel wasn't going to stop me. I'd gotten over bigger mountains than this.

"You can stay with us if you want." Lexie's offer came out of nowhere.

I turned to stare at her. Was she serious? She didn't even know me. How did I say this nicely? After what I'd learned about men in my life, then unless she was a lesbian I wasn't staying with her. "Ah, thanks, but..."

"That's a good idea, actually," Toni piped up, interrupting me.

"Lexie's place has heaps of spare bedrooms, and her men might look a bit rough, but they're as loyal as the day is long."

Men? Rough? Sorry... what?

"Did you say... men?" I asked, gaping at Toni then turning to study the seemingly normal-looking woman to my right. What had I stumbled into here?

Lexie swallowed hard and fidgeted like a toddler caught with her hand in the cookie jar. "Ah... yes. I'm in a relationship with two men, Oliver and Markus. We only take up one bedroom, so you could take any of the spares. They won't mind."

She was in a what? I suddenly had a new appreciation for the woman in front of me. To take on one of those bastards took guts. To take on two... she was a braver woman than me.

I smiled at her and tried to explain that there was no way I could impose on her. Even if she did seem to genuinely want to help me. "I appreciate the offer but..."

Toni jumped in again. "The motel is flea-bitten and any of the more expensive places will be more money than you'll make in a day."

She was right. I was fucked.

I tapped into my intuition and realized that it was only my pride stopping me from accepting the offered help. Nothing about either of these women was setting off alarm bells in my gut. And if Lexie's men were even halfway decent, I could survive a few days, surely?

I sighed heavily and finally conceded. "Um... well, I suppose I don't have much of a choice. Thank you, Lexie. Ring up the parts you need and take my credit card before I change my mind."

I unzipped one of the discreet pockets in my leather pants and pulled out my only bank card. I handed it over to Lexie, hoping they'd leave me enough to eat.

Toni waved her hand to stop the transaction. "I need to make some calls first. See where I can source these parts. How about you go get some lunch and come back afterward. Actually, Lexie, can you go pick up our orders at The Pantry?"

Lexie handed me back the card and I quickly hid it again. The wave of relief that washed over me was way more intense than it should have been.

"Sure," Lexie said, grabbing a sweater and her handbag. "Come on, Nancy. I'll walk with you."

I tied my hair back with a hairband I kept around my wrist and readied myself to face people. The only downside of riding a bike was helmet hair. But when I scraped it back like this, at least it was neat. "Okay. Thanks."

We walked out into the sunshine and I grabbed my cell phone from the saddle bag on my bike, one of the only things I owned of any value. It was switched off, of course, so no-one could trace me. But I didn't want to just leave it on the street.

"I can't believe my bad luck," I said as I stared at my broken bike. "Seriously."

Lexie shrugged and we began the walk back to the main street. "At least you're okay. The bike's fixable."

Great... she's one of those glass-half-full types.

"Yeah... but I'm down to my last few grand," I said, staring out at the road. I didn't want her to know how much this money issue stressed me, but I had to face it if I was going to get my bike fixed. "I'll have to get a job here, or something."

"What do you do?" she asked in a curious tone.

I looked up at her and grinned. "I'm a hairdresser actually. Know anyone who needs a cut?"

Lexie frowned at me. "Seriously?"

"Seriously." I burst out laughing at her surprised look, unable to help myself. "I can also waitress. Clean houses. Babysit. Probably tune a bike, but that's it for mechanic skills."

I knew I didn't look like any hairdresser anyone else had seen, but it was a tradeable skill.

Lexie stopped outside a café and opened the glass door. "I'm sure we can find something for you, then."

As I prepared to enter, two men walked out of the café and I stumbled back to give them room. Suddenly, I found it difficult to suck in a breath. They were huge. And gorgeous. And their presence made my knees begin to shake in the worst possible way.

TWO

TANNER.

Wade and I drove all night to get home. We weren't sure why, but instead of staying at a motel last night, we'd both voted to just keep going.

It was a bit strange that we'd both felt the same way because there was no real rush to get home. No event on. No calls for help. But as wolf shifters, we followed our instincts, and we didn't question a push from Fate.

So, we'd filled up the truck with gas, loaded up on food, and kept driving. All I'd been able to think was that maybe our family needed us and they hadn't yet made the call?

Our first stop once we reached town was The Pantry. We needed sustenance after driving all night, and grabbed a couple of coffees to keep us going till we reached our parents' house. We both wanted to check in with them and make sure everything was okay.

"Look who it is," Wade said, grinning as a familiar brunette opened the café door.

I strode faster toward the door and stepped through before Lexie could step in. Conversation outside in the fresh air was always better.

I smiled at her and stopped myself from grabbing her up in a hug. The new human addition to our pack wasn't quite ready for the wolfy level of affection we all usually displayed. "Thanks, cousin."

Lexie laughed and looked up at us with a sparkle in her eyes. "Hey guys. I didn't know you were back already."

I shrugged and went to answer her when my gaze was suddenly tugged toward the woman standing next to Lexie. "Yeah... we, ah... got back today."

I couldn't talk properly. I couldn't think. All I could do was stare at her. She was so beautiful!

Lexie said something, maybe to Wade, but I couldn't focus on her or her words. Her friend held my interest completely. Who was she? She had skin as pure as silk. And those curves... damn. I could get lost in those gorgeous breasts.

Lexie's voice came back into focus suddenly and I realized she'd started the introduction. "Nancy, this is Tanner and Wade. They're cousins to Ollie and Markus. Guys, this is Nancy. She just came into town and she's gonna stay with me and the boys for a bit."

This beautiful woman was staying with our cousins? A strange rumble of disapproval rolled through me.

"Guys, you're being rude," Lexie said, her voice squeaking with what sounded like excitement. "Shake Nancy's hand."

Wade was closer than me to Nancy and when he glanced across at me, I finally understood. She was our mate. The woman we'd been waiting for. Wade looked half terrified, and I knew my face most likely betrayed the same feelings.

We'd always known we'd end up with one woman between us. It was common for a perfect pair set, and we were closer and more in sync than most twins anyway.

But the reality of it finally happening was surreal.

Wade lifted his arm, ever so slowly, toward the woman in front of us. We could be wrong. There was only one way to find out, and Lexie knew what that was. We had to touch Nancy.

She glanced over at Lexie, looking just as nervous as Wade.

Lexie, God love her, elbowed Nancy in the side. "Don't worry. They won't bite."

Well...

Finally, Nancy reached out to shake Wade's hand. The moment their palms connected, Wade groaned like someone was pulling his arm out of his socket.

I reached for my brother, but stopped as Nancy's gasp rang out around us.

This was it. A pivotal moment in our life.

Wade collapsed onto his knees like someone had knocked the wind out of him.

I stared at Nancy in disbelief. Despite that gasp, she was still standing. In fact, she looked furious.

She pulled her hand out of Wade's grip and jumped back, rubbing her palm on her leather pants. "He shocked me!"

Lexie burst out with a giggle that had Nancy rounding on her with a clearly angry expression. "What the hell is going on here?"

I coughed to clear my throat. "I... ah... can probably explain that." I wanted to touch her too. Not because I wanted to get shocked onto my ass like Wade, but because I needed to know for sure.

I hauled my brother to his feet, then stepped around him. "Nancy... I..."

"Oh no, don't you touch me." She growled at me, pulling Lexie in front of her as a shield. "I've had enough of this shit! Do you understand me? I won't let another man ruin my life!"

She turned and ran away.

My jaw dropped as I watched her luscious, leather-clad figure haul ass down the street.

Lexie whacked me in the chest. "Go after her, dumb ass!"

I started jogging after Nancy and heard Lexie say to Wade. "One at a time."

So, Wade wasn't following us. No problem.

I followed Nancy back to Toni's shop where she stopped at a

beautiful pink bike. She scrabbled inside one of the saddle bags then turned quickly to face me.

I skidded in my tracks, putting the brakes on hard.

She was holding out in front of her a hunting knife the length of her forearm. "Don't come any closer. I'm not afraid to use this."

I put my hands up like I was trying to placate an offender at a bank robbery. "I won't. I'm sorry. I didn't mean to scare you."

"I'm not afraid of you," she hissed through clenched teeth. Her actions belied her words. She was obviously terrified I was about to hurt her.

Toni stepped out of the garage at that point, saw what was going on, and raced back inside. Probably for her shotgun, knowing Toni. Now I had to hurry. Toni wasn't going to go easy on Nancy.

"Listen." I took a few steps back. "You're a stranger to us, so you need to put that down. Our kind don't take lightly to our pack mates being threatened."

Nancy frowned a little. "What do you mean by that?"

Chut, chut. The sound of someone racking a shotgun was a sound most people would recognize. Including Nancy, judging by the way she immediately froze and turned around slowly. Toni had her shotgun loaded and leveled at Nancy's head.

I waved at Toni. "It's okay, Tone. Seriously. This is just a misunderstanding."

Toni didn't move and neither did Nancy.

Fucking headstrong women.

I loved them, but seriously?

I had to explain everything, fast. Before anyone got hurt. "Toni. Nancy's our fated mate. She freaked out when she shook hands with Wade and knocked the idiot on his ass. I chased her, she freaked out again, and pulled the knife. She's not going to hurt me. She just wants to make sure she can defend herself."

Toni's smile was one for the record books as she lowered the gun to point toward the ground. "Shit... Tanner. I thought this chick was about to gut you."

I raised an eyebrow. "I appreciate the vote of confidence in my fighting skills."

"You're a pussy with women," she said. "You'd never hurt her, even if she tried to kill you."

Then Toni turned around and went back to work.

Nancy's gaze shot from Toni to me, then back to Toni.

Once the mechanic disappeared, Nancy's arm dropped and by now I could see that she was shaking hard.

"What the hell is going on here?" Her voice also contained a slight tremble, and there were tears sparkling on her lashes. My heart squeezed tight in my chest.

Lexie came wandering up like she was here for a picnic. "You two okay?"

"Ah… no." I quickly explained what had happened.

Lexie's hand came up to cover her mouth. "Oh my God. That's a new one."

"I'm from the South." Nancy sniffed, wiping at the tears that had gotten through the keeper. "You're lucky I don't carry a gun."

Wade walked up behind Lexie, looking sheepish. "Everything okay?"

I ran a frazzled hand through my hair. "Ah… no. Not really."

Nancy stood up a little straighter now, her gaze going from me, to my brother. "What… Why do I…"

"Why do you think they're the hottest guys you've ever seen?" Lexie asked, her voice hopeful and bright.

Nancy looked away from all of us, her cheeks slashed with redness.

I glanced over at Wade. Good to know she actually does think we're hot, even if she threatened to stab me a few minutes ago.

"Look, I'm hungry," Lexie said. "So's Nancy. How about we go get some lunch, then I'll show her to my place so she can rest, and you guys come over for dinner maybe?"

I didn't like the sound of that. She wanted us to leave our mate now that we'd just met her? I hadn't even had the chance to touch

Nancy and confirm it properly, yet. Not that I needed the proof. I could feel the connection in my very bones.

Lexie walked over to Nancy and whispered. "Put the knife away, hon. No-one's gonna hurt you in this town."

Nancy whispered back. "What was that fated mate shit he was saying about me?"

Lexie didn't answer but at least Nancy finally put her knife away.

"I'll explain later," Lexie said.

I took a step toward them. "No, Lexie. You need to let us explain."

She crossed her arms and glared at me. "I don't think that's a good idea right now."

"Why not?" Wade asked, stepping up next to me, shoulder to shoulder.

Lexie shook her head. "You guys don't add two and two together well, do you?"

Then she sighed heavily and gestured to the bike. "Nancy's been traveling, what... three days? Longer?"

Nancy gulped. "Ah... um... six, maybe?"

Lexie turned her gaze back on us. "She's barely slept, and she's starving. She's armed and traveling alone. I hate to say it... but she's running away from something. Probably a guy, or family. Yes, Nancy?"

Lexie turned her eagle eye on our mate, who paled like she was a bottle of milk in the sun. "I... ah..."

Lexie linked her arm with our mate, showing a solid female bond already. "These guys, like my guys, might look big and rough, but they'll never hurt you. I swear to all that is holy, Nancy. In fact, you'll find that these two will very soon be the best chance you have of surviving whatever or whoever's chasing you."

Nancy's jaw dropped, as did mine.

"So it's true? You're running from someone?" I asked.

"Who?" Wade demanded. "Who hurt you?"

Lexie looked at Nancy and simply said, "See?"

I wasn't sure what she was talking about, but my hands had

closed into fists and I was just about shaking from the anger pulsing through me.

Someone had hurt my mate? A man? He was dead. So dead.

Lexie cupped her hand and whispered something into Nancy's ear that I couldn't hear over the pounding of my own heartbeat.

Nancy shook her head and whispered back. "No!"

Lexie pushed her towards me. "Do it. You'll see."

Nancy glanced back at Lexie, then slowly crept toward us. She rubbed one hand over her bare arm, shivering as she walked. "This is insane."

Lexie called out after her. "We'll go get some lunch after this."

Nancy took another step and then another, until she was within touching distance. She stared directly at me and her eyes were like warm chocolate, making me hot all over.

She sighed heavily, then stuck her hand out for me to shake. "Lexie said I have to shake your hand too, then I won't be so worried about you guys hurting me."

I shifted my gaze to my cousin's mate and yelled out, "Traitor!"

"Aw... you guys love me." She cackled.

I groaned and reached out for her small hand. "This is gonna hurt, isn't it?"

The moment our palms touched, a pulse of lightning shot up my arm and into my body. I tried to lock my knees, but there was no hope. I was going down.

My legs wobbled and I fell onto my knees, lights flashing in my head like the most brilliant of orgasms, knocking out my sight.

There was pleasure behind it all, though. A deep satisfaction of knowing I'd finally found the woman meant to be my mate, my wife.

Our wife.

Nancy let go of my hand and stared down at me. But this time, instead of running away, she just stayed there.

"I still don't get it," she whispered.

I managed to smile up at her, not even trying to get up yet. It was no use. I had no strength in my legs.

"You will," I promised.

She nodded slowly, then backed away until she stood next to Lexie once more. Safe.

"See you guys tonight," Lexie called out, waving at us and pulling Nancy out of sight.

Wade offered me a hand and hauled me to my feet, much as I'd done for him.

His smile was huge, and infectious. "We've found her, brother."

I nodded and shook off the dirt from my jeans. I wanted to go after Nancy, but deep down I knew Lexie was right. We could go round there this evening and sort things out then. "Let's go tell Mom and Dad."

Our instincts had been right. We had to come home, and we'd made it just in time, it seemed, to save our mate from whoever was chasing her.

CHAPTER

THREE

NANCY.

I let Lexie talk me into getting some lunch, then walking back to her place.

"You sure your boss, doesn't mind you leaving early?" I asked, feeling jittery and nervous after the day I'd had.

We walked up to a new-ish house, picturesque in every way. White picket fence. Blue front door. The kind of house I used to dream of living in when I was young.

"Nah. Toni's awesome," Lexie answered, walking up the path and unlocking the front door with a key from her bag. "Plus, she knows who you are, so she'll be even more relaxed if I need a few days."

"A few days for what?" I asked, following Lexie inside her home. "And what do you mean... who I am? You've really gotta start explaining to me what's going on. I feel like everyone's in the loop here, except for me."

I was trying to be assertive and slightly badass, but the house took my breath away. Everything was so big, and clean, and lush, and... "This place is amazing." I stared around with wide eyes.

"Isn't it?" she gushed, flopping down on the huge sofa and placing our lunch on the coffee table in front of her. "The guys are talking about building a bigger one, but I love it here. Come, eat."

Lexie pushed my takeaway platter of sandwiches at me.

I dropped down onto the couch opposite her. "You bought enough for three people."

She laughed. "Hardly. One of my guys would have devoured that whole plate."

She picked up her chicken roll and began eating.

I swallowed hard, my stomach rolling. I took a sip of my hot chocolate from the take away cup and picked up the sandwich. I hesitated then, knowing that once I started eating, I wasn't going to be able to stop. I didn't want to start feeling sick, or make a pig of myself.

"Go on," Lexie said. "Just eat one, if you want. I'll put the rest in the fridge for later."

I nodded and took out one sandwich, then pushed the rest away, but Lexie left them there on the table.

Once I started chewing, I was right. I couldn't stop. I moaned aloud at the taste of the chicken and mayonnaise sandwich. It was amazing. But the beef and ketchup one was even better.

"I'll get us some sodas," Lexie said at one point, getting up to go into the other room, then surfacing with a multitude of choices.

I took a Pepsi to sip on, which helped slow down my chewing.

"I had no idea I was so hungry." I leaned back on the couch to take a breath. "Thanks for that."

Lexie smiled with eyes that shone.

I groaned and looked heavenward. "Why are you looking at me like that?"

She cackled. "I'm not meant to tell you."

I gave her the evil eye. "But you're going to, aren't you?"

She opened her mouth, but didn't get the chance to answer. The front door opened and from the sound of it, more than one person walked in. Their heavy boots clumped on the floor as they stomped and pulled them off. "Lexie!" A loud voice boomed out.

She flew out of her seat and ran for them, a look of pure bliss on her face.

I got up and followed her, curious to see this.

There were two men by the front door, in jeans and dirty tank tops.

I stopped in my tracks. They were freaking huge, scary-looking dudes, and yet Lexie threw herself at them like a child.

Their faces transformed on seeing her, big smiles bursting out of them as they took turns cuddling and kissing her.

I'd never seen anything like it before.

When they finally finished kicking off their boots, Lexie tugged them toward me.

When their gazes settled on me, both of their faces grew serious. "Who have you got here?"

They were brothers, that was obvious. They didn't look much alike, but there was a kinship feel to them. Much like Tanner and Wade. One larger and darker, one smaller and lighter. But both simultaneously sexy. And yet, I couldn't help but compare them to Tanner and Wade. Those two at the café had been a whole other level of sexy.

"Guys, this is Nancy. Her bike broke down as she was passing through town, and it's at Toni's shop. I told her she could stay here for a few days."

"Of course," the blonder guy said, and slung an arm over Lexie's shoulders. "But what are we missing?"

"Nancy," Lexie continued. "This is Oliver and Markus." She indicated to the two guys and I nodded politely.

Then she cupped her hand and whispered into the blond guy's ear.

I groaned, getting annoyed now. "Stop fucking doing that! We're not in high school."

Lexie turned to me and glared. "You're no fun."

I threw my hands up and marched back to the couch where I started eating again.

The guys came over, smiled and headed toward the kitchen. "We've actually gotta head back to work. Just popped in for some lunch."

"There's dinner leftovers in the fridge," Lexie called after them.

I watched the exchange with interest. They were obviously in love, all three of them.

"So... you're with both of them?" I asked, unable to keep my curiosity at bay. "Like... equally?"

She nodded and reached for her soda can. "Yep. Same bed. Every night."

"But they don't..." I made a gesture with my hands and she made a gagging sound.

"Of course not. Gross. They're twins."

"Twins?" I repeated. "I mean, they do look like brothers, but they're quite different from each other." Kind of like Tanner and Wade, my traitorous brain whispered again.

The guys ambled back into the room, a plate of meat and vegetables in front of each of them. They walked around the coffee table, set down their food, and sat on either side of Lexie.

Well... they were practically on top of her. As close as possible while still being able to eat.

"Whatcha talking about?" Oliver asked, chomping on something loud. A carrot maybe.

"Perfect pairs," Lexie answered, grinning at me.

"Perfect what?" I asked, not sure what topic we were on now.

"You sure you should be telling her everything?" Markus said, grabbing a can of drink from the table. "Her guys might wanna fill her in."

"Oh please." Lexie rolled her eyes. "I wish someone had told me about you guys beforehand. I'm just gonna give her a heads up."

"Okay. Your call." Markus shrugged his massive shoulders.

I sat back and had a good look at the trio. Lexie was gorgeous, of course. But not in a traditional way. She was chubby, like me. Big boobs, decent sized ass, though I was definitely bigger than her.

Whereas these guys? They were billboard material. Gorgeous faces, perfect bodies. What the hell was in the water around here?

Even the fact that the guys deferred to her judgment was amazing to me. No man in my family would ever have let a woman tell him he was wrong. Let alone allow a woman to ride over his opinion in the way Lexie had just done to her two.

But they looked happier than pigs in mud, eating their leftovers and cuddling into their woman.

Lexie grinned at me as though she'd caught me staring. Truth was, she had. "It's weird, huh?"

I gulped, then reached for my drink. "What is?"

"This." She gestured to the guys beside her.

I smiled hesitantly. She didn't know much about me. I didn't want her to think that I was being too judgy. "Oh, it's not the two guys thing. You do you. Whatever makes you happy."

She nodded, her eyes burning with intensity as she stared at me. "Yeah, I know. It's their devotion, their acceptance, their love. Isn't it?"

Now my face was burning up with heat. "Ah..."

"I think that's our cue to head off," Oliver said, grabbing his plate and standing up. "You want take-out for dinner?"

Lexie shrugged. "Sure. Message me later? We may have a couple of extra guests for dinner."

He nodded and dropped a kiss on her lips before turning to me. "See you tonight."

I managed to smile at him and waited while the guys cleaned up after themselves and left, going back to work for the day.

I stared after them. "They're..."

"Amazing, I know," Lexie finished for me. "I didn't know guys could even do dishes."

I huffed out a laugh. "Yeah. In my family, they don't."

They didn't cook, or clean, or wash, or help with kids. That was considered woman's work.

Lexie settled back on the couch and lifted her chin. "Shoot. Ask your questions. I know you have some."

I crossed my legs, then winced. These leather pants were great for keeping my skin on if I came off my bike. Not so great for relaxing on someone's comfortable sofa.

"Hey, you got a change of clothes?" Lexie asked. "Or do you want a spare pair of tights and a T-shirt?"

"I have clothes in the bag with my bike," I said, though the clothes in question weren't exactly clean. I hadn't stopped anywhere long enough to do a wash.

She waved her hand. "Come with me."

I followed her to a huge bedroom where she rummaged through some drawers before she led me to a lovely white, modern bathroom. "Look, I'm not going anywhere, so there's no rush on this conversation. Have a shower. Get changed. I'll be downstairs when you're ready to chat. And that bedroom there," she pointed to the one next to the one we were in, "is my old room. So, if you want to lie down for a few hours, I wouldn't blame you."

Her kindness stepped over the walls I'd raised up around my heart and made tears well in my eyes. "It's too much. I can't intrude…"

"Of course, you can." She pushed the clothes at me and pointed to a heavenly fluffy towel. "Everything you need is in here. Help yourself."

She turned to walk away and I touched her on the shoulder to make her turn back around.

"Lexie, why are you doing this? You don't know me. I could steal all your stuff. Or…"

She reached out and held my hand, squeezing my fingers tight. "Nancy, look, I know what it's like to not know where your next meal is coming from. I know what it's like to feel… worthless. Fat. Ugly. Unlovable."

I dropped my head and stared down at the ground.

She shook my hand a little. "Hey... I didn't mean to infer anything about you, I just... look. I'm the first person to judge and be critical, or I was, anyway. But these guys have changed me, and if there's any true justice in the world, or karma? Let's just say, I'm passing it along."

I took my hand back, unwilling to admit how close to the truth she'd gotten. "Thank you."

She grinned. "I'm gonna go get a few things done downstairs since we're having guests for dinner now. You shower, rest, whatever you want. See you downstairs when you're ready, okay?"

I nodded and Lexie disappeared down the hallway.

I took a deep, steadying breath. Was this real? Or was I dreaming? Maybe I was dead... maybe I'd crashed my bike along the road somewhere.

I lifted my arm and pinched myself, hard. "Ow."

Okay, so maybe I wasn't dead. I walked into the bathroom and locked the door. Not that I didn't trust Lexie, but the old saying was true. Old habits die hard.

I stripped off my sweaty, sticky clothes and folded them into a dark pile on the clean white tiles. They looked wrong. Totally wrong.

But I didn't let the swirly feeling in my gut make me grab my clothes and run like it was telling me to. That wasn't intuition. It was just fear. It was hard to tell the difference sometimes, but in this moment I knew which was which.

I stepped into the over-sized shower, flicked on the hot water and closed my eyes as the heavenly heat rained down on my body and face.

I turned, letting the showerhead massage the kinks from my shoulders and wash the dirt out of my hair. I reached for the shampoo and finally, didn't try and stop the tears that welled and fell. It was safe to let it all out in this space. And when a sob rose in my throat, I let it out. Then found myself laughing as well as crying.

I hadn't felt this safe in so long. And the fact that I was standing naked, in the shower of a complete stranger's house, made the whole situation even funnier.

What did it say about my past that this moment made me feel loved, and every minute of my life before now had made me feel the complete opposite?

FOUR

WADE.

I was itching to see our mate again. I could barely wait to get on over to Lexie's place. "Come on. Come on," I called out to my brother, for probably the tenth time. The asshole was changing his shirt—again. "She won't care what you're bloody wearing!"

She wouldn't. I knew it. Just like we wouldn't care if she was wearing a hessian sack. Nancy was still the most beautiful woman I'd ever seen, and I could not wait to strip her naked and get her into bed.

"Fine. Let's go," Tanner said, stomping into the living room, his shirt still unbuttoned. "You know it's only, like, five thirty?"

I already had my keys and phone in my pocket. "Yeah, and?"

"We were invited for dinner. Even six o'clock would be considered a stretch."

I didn't want to listen. Fuck Tanner. I wanted my mate. Now. Hell, I wanted her five years ago. I yanked open the front door and stomped to the truck. We were nearly forty, for fuck's sake. Why had Fate taken this long to send us our woman? Sleeping around and having fun had gotten old ten years ago.

Tanner locked up and headed to the truck, doing up the last of his buttons before jumping in. "Just relax, bro. She's not going anywhere. At least for the next few days."

I glared at him while simultaneously turning on the engine. "She's passing through. Her plans are to leave as soon as Toni fixes her bike. Don't tell me to relax."

I twisted the wheel and hit the gas, speeding out of our building's driveway faster than I should have.

Tanner chuckled, low and amused. "So, we follow her, to the ends of the earth if need be. Don't worry, brother. I'm not letting her go, either. Not now that she's finally come into our lives."

I glanced across at my twin and finally saw what I wanted to see. Determination. Not as obvious or aggressive as mine was, but it was there. Beneath the relaxed features, my brother was as set on this path as I was.

My whole body immediately relaxed. "Good."

We drove to Markus and Ollie's home, getting there in less than five minutes. I was out of the car before the engine cooled and raced up to the front door.

Tanner was close on my heels, still chuckling. "You know we could have walked."

I didn't answer him, instead choosing to knock on the front door. I knew we could have walked here, and it might have almost been faster. Hell, I would have shifted and run, arriving naked if I thought it would have helped us get Nancy. But our mate was skittish, and human, and the last thing I wanted to do was alert her to the fact that we weren't.

Skittish, or human.

At least, not yet.

The door opened wide and there was Lexie, standing on the other side with a big grin on her face. "You beat my boys home."

She stepped back and waved us in. "They're picking up takeaway on the way. Hope you guys are hungry. I ordered enough for a small army."

We stepped into the lovely bright living room, a sudden weirdness passing over me. Lexie was being nice, as always, which was at odds with the hot blood pumping through my veins.

I forced myself to nod, glancing around for Nancy. "Yeah, we're always hungry."

"Thanks, Lex," Tanner added, catching my eye and glaring at me. I was sure he could feel my tension rising. Hell, he was probably feeling exactly the same.

Lexie laughed and patted me on the arm. "It's all good. I can only imagine how stressful this is for you guys. Come in, have a beer."

"Where is she?" I asked, unable to move forward until I knew that my mate was safe, and preferably within arm's reach.

"She's still upstairs," Lexie said, gesturing to the staircase near the front door. "She had a shower and a nap. I woke her up a few minutes ago, but you'll need to give her some time to come downstairs and join us. She was running on empty before."

My knees unlocked and I managed to walk forward again on the plush carpet they'd installed. "Is she okay?"

We followed Lexie into the kitchen where she offered us a beer and waved at a platter of meat and cheese on the countertop. "Help yourselves." I stared at her, wanting an answer. She grinned at me, taking a sip of her water before answering. "She's okay, I think."

"You think?" I repeated, not sure what that meant.

Lexie shrugged again, acting way happier than she should be at this point in time. Didn't she realize how important this was?

I growled at her, not really meaning to.

That's when she snapped at me. "Hey! Rein it in. I know you've been waiting for your fated mate for a while..."

"Try decades," I corrected her.

"Well, don't blame me for that!" she yelled, putting her hands on her hips. "Stop it? Okay? That woman up there is freaked out, running from some asshole she hasn't named yet, and has never heard of anything even remotely like a shifter. So fucking calm down, because I can tell you, your road isn't going to be easy."

The front door opened and a male voice boomed out. Markus. "Yo! We're home!"

Lexie's face lit up with happiness at hearing her mate's voice. Then she schooled her features once more. "Excuse me." She walked calmly toward the front door, breaking into a run when she neared them.

Tanner glanced over at me. "I'm staying here. Those three are too happy."

I snorted. "Yeah I know. They make me sick, too."

The sound of a soft moan hit my ears.

I called out. "Hey, hey, hey... Keep it PG."

One of the guys chuckled from the other room and I decided it was probably safe to move now. Tanner and I strolled into the living room. There, the scene was less hot than expected. Lexie and Markus were still cuddling but Oliver was unpacking the food onto the dining room table.

"Come grab a plate," Oliver called, gesturing to us.

There was a stack of plastic plates on the table next to a bunch of Thai take away containers.

"Smells great," said a soft female voice from the doorway.

I turned to stare as Nancy's voice announced her arrival. She was wearing a comfortable pair of leggings and a T-shirt that clung to the curves of her breasts.

She tugged at the T-shirt awkwardly. "It's Lexie's. It's a bit tight."

I couldn't speak all of a sudden, but managed a smile somehow. I glanced at Wade and saw him staring at Nancy too. Neither of us seemed to be capable of speaking.

She was fucking gorgeous, and I wanted nothing more than to sweep her up into my arms and hold her tight.

"You look great," Lexie said in lieu of our response. She grabbed hold of Nancy's hand and drew her closer. "Come eat."

Lexie began cracking open containers of food and my stomach growled. It had been a long time since lunch and I was starving, but I couldn't stop looking at our mate. At her lush curves, and her long hair with lovely red and gold highlights throughout. She was freshly showered and smelled of flowers.

I only just stopped myself from rushing over and pressing my nose to her neck. I wanted to inhale every bit of her. I wanted to wrap myself around her and never let her go. But I knew it was too early to show anything like that.

"Drinks, everyone?" Markus called out. "I'll get a stack from the fridge. Sit. Eat."

Nancy had gotten a plate and taken a seat at the other end of the table. Tanner rushed to scoop a whole lot of rice and chicken onto his plate, then scooch down to sit next to her.

"Come on, Wade," Lexie said. "You're gonna miss out. This satay sauce is amazing."

I forced my legs to work and walked forward to take the plate Lexie had made for me. She handed me a fork and, with a roll of her eyes, shoved me along the table toward Nancy.

I sat next to Tanner, not wanting to surround our new mate and overwhelm her.

Lexie sat next to Nancy, who shot her new friend a grateful smile.

Lexie tore apart some roti bread and dabbed it in the peanut sauce. "So, Nancy, tell us who you're running from."

Nancy's eyes widened at the statement. She picked up her fork and shoveled some fried rice into her mouth.

I glared at Lexie. "Subtle much?"

She laughed. "I'm sorry. Have you met me?"

Markus came back from the kitchen and put a stack of cans on the table, mostly soda. "You guys want beers too?"

Tanner answered for us. "Nah, this is great. Thanks, guys."

"Anytime," Markus said, coming around the table to kiss his mate on the top of the head before he made himself a plate.

I stared at him for probably too long because he shot me a look. "What?"

"Nothing," I managed to spit out. "It's just, I didn't notice before how much you don't give Lexie her own space."

Nancy chuckled, getting my attention immediately. "Right? They practically sit on top of her."

Tanner laughed. "Yeah, well, it's better than how they were before they met Lexie. Moping about, all lonely and shit."

"Markus wasn't lonely!" Lexie all but exploded from the other side of the table. "He was still sleeping with…"

Markus groaned and headed off for more food.

"He was dating someone when you met?" Nancy asked.

"Well, I wouldn't call it dating…" Lexie rolled her eyes.

Nancy dragged her gaze up to meet mine and I could finally see the vulnerability that Lexie had been talking about. Back at the café she had presented as a typical tough biker chick. Here… she was totally different.

"Are you two… with anyone?" she asked, directing her query to me and Tanner.

I held up my hands, "Hell no. Single as the day is long."

"Me too," Tanner added. "We're ten years older than our cousins over there. We aren't looking for casual shit anymore. Haven't been for a long time."

Nancy nodded and dropped her gaze back to her food.

Markus started asking questions about our latest trip and the work we'd been doing, and we returned the favor, asking them about the latest house they were building. The conversation flowed easily and I ate my fill, darting glances at Nancy throughout.

By the time we were all done and the plates were in the trash, I was more relaxed than I'd been in ages.

Nancy leaned back and patted her belly. "Wow. I can't believe how much I ate."

Her breasts were huge, jutting out loud and proud within her stretched thin T-shirt. I had to stifle the groan that rose as lust kicked me in the groin. Damn, I wanted her. If—no, when—I had the chance, I'd spend hours on those nipples alone.

"Come sit on the couches for a while," Lexie said, gesturing to us. "But fair warning. We go to bed at, like, eight-thirty. Like grandmas."

I glanced at the wall clock above the fireplace mantel. It was around seven so we still had time before they'd disappear.

"Yeah, but not to sleep," Oliver said, slapping his mate on the ass, then crash-tackling her to the couch.

I stood up and watched the bonded triad fight over which two inches they wanted to all fit on.

I glanced over at Nancy. "I say we let them all get comfy first, then we try and find a spot to sit."

She grinned at me, seeming more comfortable around us now. "Smart move."

When Markus and Ollie finally stopped fighting over which part of Lexie they got to hold, the rest of us ventured over to the remaining sofas.

Nancy sat by herself on an edge of the couch the others were snuggled on, so Tanner and I took the larger sofa so we could still look at our mate but not crowd her too much.

"So?" Lexie said, sitting on Markus's lap. "Nancy. You gonna tell us what you're running from? After all, if you're staying here, it's probably best if we know what might walk through our door."

Nancy tucked her legs up and wrapped her arms around her knees. "I'll leave before anything comes this way, Lexie. Don't worry."

Lexie's laugh was adorable, but my blood was beginning to boil. What had happened to our mate to make her so concerned about everyone's safety?

I glanced at Markus, whose ears were pricked as well. He met my gaze. We didn't carry guns, or other weapons. We had our fangs and claws and could shift in moments. But what if that wasn't enough?

"Nancy?" I spoke in a low, coaxing tone. "Please tell us."

It was killing me not knowing. Was this one of those moments when the situation had been blown out of proportion? Or was it the other way around? I didn't know Nancy well enough to be able to read her, but she didn't look like one of those girls who cried wolf.

"Um..." Nancy blew out a breath, shook herself, then pushed her legs down so that her feet were now flat on the carpet. "You're right. Toni's not fixing my bike tonight, so…"

She began to shiver, and I couldn't just sit there and let her combust.

I stood up and gestured to the Lexie pile of people. "Shove over."

Then I jammed myself into the space between the triad and Nancy. Markus and Olliver grumbled but eventually moved over.

I didn't touch Nancy, even though I wanted to. But I was there if she needed me and I hoped that she could sense that.

When she lifted her gaze to mine and a tiny smile quivered on her lips, I knew that she felt my care.

"Go," I said, nodding at her. "Whatever it is, we've got you."

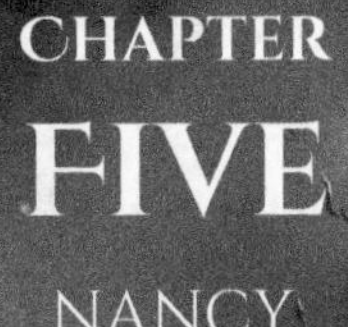

CHAPTER
FIVE

NANCY.

As soon as Wade sat next to me, my system calmed. Which was the complete opposite to what I'd expected. He was way too big, and attractive for me to feel comfortable around, and yet, my breathing began to slow and even out the longer he sat there.

Lexie was right. I had to tell them who was coming after me. They didn't need to know all the gory details, but the gist was probably enough. "I don't want to get any of you in trouble, so I'll tell you. Yes, I'm running away. To the only place I know that's safe, my uncle's ranch. It's a few days' ride from here."

"We could drive you," Tanner said suddenly, and then Wade waved his hand at his brother.

"Yeah, we could. But let her finish her story first."

I couldn't help but smile at the brothers' tones. They would fight like cat and dog on days, I was sure. But the kinship was there; the love, the loyalty... that was clearly deep and genuine. And it was nice to be around after all the shit I'd put up with.

"Okay. So, long story short. My dad was a biker. An eight-one. He kept me out of the club as much as he could, but I had to go in and drag his ass out on occasion. Then, last year, he died, and some of the club boys started hanging around the house. Wanting to help, they said."

I gulped as emotions that I'd been pushing down for too long began to surface. "Um..."

Wade reached out and squeezed my leg, gently, sending a shock through me that made me yelp. "Holy moly, what is that?"

Wade withdrew his hand, groaning as though he was in pain.

I looked over at Lexie. "Am I, like, electrocuting them?"

Oliver laughed uproariously. "Yeah, pretty much. But another time or two and it'll disappear."

Wade exhaled slowly, his body shuddering for a moment before his shoulders dropped and relaxed once more. "Sorry. I'm good. Keep going."

I didn't know why it seemed so much worse for Tanner and Wade than me, but I slid a few inches further away.

Wade looked crushed, his eyes shadowing with pain. I glanced away, not wanting to see it. Not wanting to try and figure out what it all meant.

"Keep going," Lexie invited. "You're safe here."

And unbelievably, I actually felt safe. I had since the moment I got here.

"Okay, well... um, I kinda fell for one of the guys. Travis. He's exactly what my parents tried to keep me away from."

"What's he into?" Tanner asked from the sofa across the room.

"Everything," I managed, though there was a lump in my throat the size of a fist. "Drugs... weapons..."

"Did he hurt you?" Tanner growled at me.

I shivered but not with fear. The sounds they made were strangely comforting. "Um... yes? No? I..."

"It's okay," Wade said quietly, not reaching out to touch me, though I felt his desire to. "You can tell us."

I wiped at the tears that fell on my cheeks. "He, um... I broke up with him last week and he went crazy. Saying I was his property and I couldn't leave him."

A sob caught in my throat with the memory. It had been a lot worse than that, of course. But I'd managed to get away. I'd grabbed what cash I had, a few clothes, and jumped on my bike. My dad's brother was the only family I had left, and he wasn't into the MC lifestyle. He was a dentist.

"You loved him?" Wade asked, his voice cracking.

I shook my head. "No. I didn't. He was just a way to get over losing my dad, I think. And you know what the worst thing was?" This part always made me laugh. "He said that he didn't love me, either. But my dad had cred, and if he was with me, it made him look better."

He'd never wanted me. In fact, he'd told me he hated having to sleep with someone as fat as me, but the club praised him so he put up with me.

Anything for the eight-ones.

I looked up at sudden movement. Lexie and her boys stood up and began to head toward the stairs. "We're gonna get an early night, but if you need us, we're upstairs. Okay?"

I nodded at her and they disappeared.

Wade was already sitting next to me, but when Tanner walked over, Wade moved across, and so did I, making room for Wade to sit on my other side.

I was the rose between the thorns. The piggie in the middle. A strangely hysterical laugh bubbled up inside me. "What's happening?"

"Um..." Tanner cleared his throat.

"Are you two gonna tell me what's going on here?"

Wade sat forward and looked over me at his brother. I didn't think they were communicating telepathically, but it was clear they were communicating.

"Hey, come on," I said, standing up and turning around so that I could look between them both more easily. The couch wasn't designed to have a three-way conversation in a line.

"Tell me."

"I have the feeling you're not gonna like it," Wade said. "I'm not sure we should tell you yet."

I laughed, feeling strangely lightheaded after revealing my sins. "Look, in this moment I feel better than I have in a year. So, this is your chance. Tell me what this thing is that I feel between us. The literal electricity every time we touch."

Wade sat back further in his place on the couch, then nodded once. "Okay. So, you're our fated mate. Which is like our soul mate."

I glanced at Tanner, the gorgeous blond one. "You mean..."

Tanner nodded. "Yes. You're meant to be with both of us. Like Lexie is with her two."

I stumbled backwards, my knees threatening to fail as my legs wobbled.

"You okay?" Tanner jumped to his feet and grabbed my arm to steady me.

A tingle of pleasure flooded me at his touch. I let him grab me. In fact, I stepped into him. I couldn't seem to help myself. "You're actually serious, aren't you?"

He stared down at me with those big, soulful blue eyes, and nodded.

I laughed and took a step back, out of his arms. "Are you fucking kidding me! Look at me." I gestured down to my huge thighs and massive tits. "And look at you! You're bloody perfect. You both are."

This was pissing me off. "Men like you don't want women like me. My ex told me exactly that. I'm fat, and ugly. I'm a pity fuck, nothing more."

There were tears in my eyes now and the self-hatred spewing from my lips made me even angrier.

When Tanner made a strangled noise and pulled me toward him, all I could see was pity. "Don't look at me like that." I covered my face with my hands, then managed to evade his embrace and raced in the direction of the stairs.

Somehow Wade moved faster. He met me at the base of the stairs and pulled me into his rock-hard body. "Why are you running from us? And why are you spewing lies about yourself? You can't believe them?"

He was staring at me with an intensity that had my belly quivering. "Ah..." Where did I even begin to explain?

"You don't think I really want you?" He growled down at me, his gaze fixed on my lips.

"No," I whispered, biting my suddenly dry lips. "You couldn't."

His hands slid around my waist and his fingers curved around my ass cheeks. "Wanna bet?"

He pulled me into him so roughly I tilted off balance and had to grab onto his huge arms. His muscles bulged beneath my fingers and I couldn't stop myself from gasping at the sudden heat between us.

"Kiss me," he demanded, staring down at me. "Show me you can feel this, too."

I lifted my chin, bringing our mouths a few inches closer together. But I didn't have the chance to kiss him as he asked. His lips crashed down on mine, sending a wave of tingly perfection through my whole body.

I moaned against his mouth and slid my fingers into his thick, dark hair. He tasted of the Thai food we'd just eaten and something darker, smokier. I opened my lips beneath the pressure of his tongue, allowing him access.

Despite the fact that the rational part of my brain still couldn't understand how a man this sexy, fit and perfect could want a woman like me, my body knew what was happening. His cock was thick and hard and pressing against my belly, through his jeans. That wasn't fake.

"My turn," Tanner said from somewhere to my right.

Wade lifted his head and turned me to face Tanner, who was waiting for me. He reached over and cupped my cheeks, leaning in and kissing me with so much tenderness I couldn't help but moan with pleasure.

Tanner's hands stayed at my face, stroking my cheek and cupping the back of my head. Their styles of kissing were polar opposites, and yet I loved both. Hot and intense, and sweet enough to break my heart. What more could a girl want than that?

When Tanner finally lifted his head I swayed on my feet. I had to be dreaming. Because only in my most secret, naughty dreams would I have imagined that two guys would want me. Two hot and sexy, amazingly good-looking, and obviously decent guys.

Maybe I'd fallen off my motorbike and I was in a coma somewhere? Maybe I'd died and gone to heaven?

I forced my eyes open and cold reality rushed back like a tidal wave. There hadn't been any major accident. I was still in this tiny town, with two strangers, and they'd just kissed me. Both of them had.

Well, I wasn't going to make this mistake again. I'd never fall for another guy's bullshit and lies. And yes, these two were convincing but there was no way I could allow myself to believe them. It would hurt too much when the truth came out.

I brought up the walls around my heart high and hard. I took a step back, trembling as I did so. My breath was coming hard and my nipples were tight and pressing against my T-shirt. Tanner and Wade both looked like they were in a similar state.

Their chests rose up and down as though they were panting, and Tanner's hands were clenched into tight fists.

No.

No.

I shook my head and stumbled up the first couple of stairs. "Let yourselves out. Please."

"Nancy, please..." Tanner reached for me with an outstretched hand.

I turned and ran for my room, terrified out of my mind. My heart was in danger again, the stupid thing believing in the passion of Tanner and Wade's kisses. But I was no fool.

Once bitten, twice shy. And I'd been bitten more than once before.

It was time to run. Again.

SIX

WADE.

I gaped at Nancy's fleeing form as she ran up the stairs and away from us. My shifter howled inside my mind as our mate got further away. "No."

Tanner grabbed my arm before I could take a step forward. "Don't go after her. You can't."

"But..."

"No," Tanner said, stronger this time. "She doesn't trust men, and she doesn't trust us. You can't rush up there and prove her right."

I gulped and nodded, stumbling toward the front door. That had gone so much worse than I'd anticipated, with her running away. And in a strange way, it had gone better than I'd ever imagined. She'd confided in us about her past and let us both kiss her. That kiss had been way hotter than anything I've experienced before.

Despite wanting to rush after Nancy and comfort her, or continue where we'd left off with that kiss, I heeded Tanner's warning. We exited the house, locking the door behind us as Lexie had told us to do.

But we didn't leave. Instead, we sat in the truck out the front, in silence. What if Nancy decided that she wanted to yell at us again? Or needed us for some reason. I couldn't bring myself to go far from her. And Tanner seemed to feel the same way since he sat in the passenger seat, as unmoving as I was.

After what felt like hours, my phone pinged with a message. I grabbed for it, though I quickly tamped down the sudden excitement when I realized it couldn't be Nancy. She didn't have my phone number.

"It's Markus," I said, opening the text and reading it quickly before putting the keys in the ignition and turning on the engine. "He said Nancy's okay, but it's probably best if we leave."

Everything inside me screamed no at that idea. My wolf was howling, desperate for his mate. But my cousin had already gone through this, and against all of my base instincts, I had to trust his advice.

"You think Markus is right?" Tanner asked, his voice stretched thin.

"Yes," I admitted, pulling the truck onto the road and heading in the direction of home. "Do I like it? Hell no. But..."

"Yeah..." Tanner agreed, before groaning loudly and tipping his head back against the seat head rest.

My brother didn't usually express his emotions the same way I did. He was calmer than me most times. Often just plain... happier. But I could tell when he wasn't feeling right, and the tension he was holding in his taut body appeared to be as bad as mine.

"You wanna go for a run?" I asked, driving straight rather than turning left into our street.

Tanner shifted in his seat to face me. "You mean, in the forest?"

"Yeah, why not? We're home." We shifted into our wolves less often than most of our pack, due to the fact that we traveled a lot. Being on the road, we'd basically gotten used to not enjoying the freedom that being in our wolf body gave us.

"Sure," he said, an element of uncertainty in his tone. It wasn't as natural as breathing for us, the way it was with most shifters.

When I thought about why, I realized there was a sadistic element to our restriction, because it hurt us not to shift regularly. Maybe we thought we didn't deserve the freedom of a shift?

"Hey," I said to Tanner as we parked on the street closest to the forest and I turned off the truck's engine. "I know we chose the road life, but do you ever miss being home? Being able to shift and run whenever you want?"

Tanner took his cell phone out of his pocket and slid it into the glove compartment. "Yeah, of course. Why?"

"Then why didn't you say anything?"

Tanner shrugged. "Coz it didn't really matter before. We were working, together. You know." He opened the door and slid out.

I threw my own cell phone under the seat, got out, then hid the keys behind the back tyre. The forest was where all of our pack ran. It wasn't a full moon but that didn't matter; we could shift anytime. In fact, there was barely a sliver of silver in the sky. And yet, I could feel my wolf stretching inside of me. Aching with the need to run.

Desperate to do it more.

"Maybe we should do this more often?" I spoke as my brother tugged off his shirt and folded it on the truck hood.

He groaned. "Wade, stop, okay? We made our choices and we've dealt with the pros and cons. But if you're asking me if I'd trade life on the road for a nice house in town with our mate? Yeah, of course I would. But what was the point setting up a home without a woman to share it with? You know how long we waited for our mate."

And that was the heart of our problem. We'd stayed around town until we were thirty, hoping that she'd show up. Hoping we could stay in town and fit into our family like everyone else, even though every day our hopes for our mate finally turning up were dashed. Over and over. As our friends married and had kids, we'd been left wondering if we'd ever find our beautiful mate.

And our hope had slowly been ground into dust.

Until Nancy. My wolf stretched and growled, wanting to be free, and suddenly I couldn't wait to let my shifter out. "Come on, brother. Let's go."

Tanner shifted into his wolf, his jeans pooling into a puddle on the concrete.

I closed my eyes and took a deep breath of the fresh air that surrounded us. I focused on the scents and sensations, the pine needles and the cold breeze. I'd shut down so many of my wolf instincts over the years, it felt almost foreign to me now.

Tanner turned tail and took off into the forest. I glanced around. There was no-one here to see us except for two houses, both owned by wolf shifter families.

I tugged my own shirt off and kicked my shoes into the dirt. Despite my wolf's eagerness to run, a shiver of unease rippled through me. For the first time in a long time, I didn't know what the future held.

I closed my eyes and let my humanity go. My wolf surged up inside of me and took over my body. My legs and arms shortened and sprouted fur, my eyes shifted to better night vision and my sense of smell heightened.

I was now on all fours, the dirt beneath my paws. Tanner howled ahead, and my ears pricked up at the sound. I took off, running toward the safety of the trees.

My heart was aching even more in this form, and even though it hurt, I tried not to fight the feelings. We'd found our mate, and even though she wasn't certain about us at the moment, surely we could convince her that we loved her and that we'd treat her like the precious and very special gift she was?

We had time. Hopefully.

❧

Nancy.

I had to get out of here. I couldn't stay in this house, or in this town.

43

After I'd run upstairs, Lexie had come in to check on me. I'd managed to reassure her that I was okay, and she'd gone back to bed.

The boys had sat in the truck for too long, looking, if I was honest, devastated. I'd watched them surreptitiously from behind my bedroom curtain. They didn't speak, but instead just stared out the windscreen with sadness tugging at their features.

I'd rushed to the shower to have a final wash, then packed my dirty clothes into a bag, left a twenty for Lexie to cover the old leggings and T-shirt I was leaving in, and pulled on my leather jacket.

I couldn't wait for Toni to fix my bike. These guys were just... no. I wasn't getting sucked into another toxic relationship, and especially not with two guys who looked so damn sweet and sexy. They'd show their true colors soon enough, and then my heart would break. I had to protect myself from that pain.

I shook my head, unable to believe that those two men wanted to share me. Me!

That was just fucked up. Even if Lexie could do it with her two guys, that wasn't me. No.

As soon as I was ready I glanced out the window and saw that the boys had finally left. I turned my cell phone on and found a bus timetable. There was one bus due through tonight, amazingly.

I ran, following the directions on my phone's map app to find a large blue bus idling at the nearby stop.

Thank God. A little bit of luck.

I paid for my ticket and climbed on board, still shaking from the adrenaline and fear coursing through my veins. I'd believed going to stay with Lexie would be safe, and okay. Instead, I'd landed in some sort of weird reverse sister wives' situation and I wasn't sure how I felt about that.

"Last call," the bus driver sang out, and I closed my eyes, pressing my forehead against the cold window. I'd have to send Toni money and come back and get my bike. Or maybe... oh, I didn't know. All I knew was that I didn't feel safe, and the only place I would, was at my uncle's house. None of Dad's old club members knew about him, so they wouldn't be able to find me.

The bus doors shut. I sat up straighter in my seat near the back. The bus vibrated beneath me as the engine revved up. I should have felt relieved, but instead there was a sinking feeling in my gut, like I was making a bad personal decision, and the bottom dropped out of my belly.

I took out my phone and stared down at the screen. Message after message dinged. All from my ex. I didn't want to open any of them. He would be looking for me, and cursing me for getting away. I just knew it.

I turned off the phone and put it down on the seat next to me. I was doing the right thing, wasn't I? Did I really want to leave my bike here? Everything I owned was in the bag beside me, or I'd left in my saddle bags on the bike.

The bus began to reverse out of its parking spot and panic hit me at a level unlike anything I'd ever felt before. I was doing the wrong thing. I knew it as surely as I'd known that running away from Travis had been the right thing for me. Leaving now was the wrong move.

The bus pulled out onto the main road and began to accelerate.

My heart was pounding and nausea hit me hard and fast. I had no idea what was happening, but I was about to throw up. And I simply had to get off this bus.

"Stop! Please!" I called out to the driver, who thankfully signaled and pulled over.

I raced to the front of the bus. "Open the doors. I'm going to be sick."

The driver acted fast, obviously not wanting someone to be ill in his vehicle. He quickly pulled the lever and the door popped open. I bolted down the stairs, dry heaving. But the moment I stepped onto solid ground, my belly stopped churning and my system calmed.

Huh. Weird.

I took some deep breaths, enjoying the cold air on my face and arms.

"Are you all right?" the bus driver called out, concern written in the angle of his eyebrows as he stared at me.

"Yeah, I am now." I waved to him. "Thanks, but I think I'm gonna stay here a few more days."

He shrugged. "Suit yourself." Then he pulled the doors shut and the bus rolled out of town. I watched it leave, feeling happier and healthier with every passing moment.

I exhaled slowly, then turned and started the walk back to Lexie's house. Luckily, we'd walked the same route this afternoon and I was pretty sure I could remember where to go even though it was dark.

I was one block away from Lexie's house when I heard a wolf howl in the distance. Goosebumps popped up on my flesh and my heart began to pump a little faster. I hurried along the next street and had finally reached Lexie's house when movement down the street caught my eye.

I stopped and looked in that direction, beneath the lamps that lit up the sidewalk. There on the path, were two wild animals. Large gray wolves. Staring straight at me. I froze, fear pumping through me.

Then, the strangest thing happened. The two wolves lay down on the path and rested their heads on their paws, gazing at me like a pair of sweet puppy dogs. I stared for a moment, a sense of calm washing over me. I felt the need to rush over and sink my fingers into their beautiful fur.

Then I shook my head, and raced for Lexie's front door, my heart pounding.

What were they doing in town? And why did I want to go to them?

I knocked on the door, hard. "Lexie!"

My chest hurt and I realized I was holding my breath. I forced myself to breathe, in, and out.

The door finally opened and Markus stood there, his huge chest blocking the doorway. His eyebrows rose when he saw me. "Nancy?"

Lexie pushed her big man mountain out of the way. "Let her in."

Markus stepped back, his surprise obvious in his expression. He wore a pair of black boxers, but nothing else.

I slipped inside and shut the door, my heart still racing.

"Ah... care to explain?" Lexie said.

I turned and faced her. She was staring at me, her hands on her hips.

"Um..."

Lexie patted Markus on the arm, "Go back to bed, hon. I've got this."

Markus grunted, turned away, and padded back upstairs.

Lexie led me over to the couch. She was dressed in only a light dressing gown and I could tell she was naked underneath. "You're lucky he bothered to put on any clothes at all. Those boys come from a naked-loving family."

I nodded, beginning to shiver. "My family wasn't like that."

Lexie laughed. "Yeah, mine either. But it's amazing how quickly you get used to it."

I sat down on the couch, truly shaking now. Lexie stood up, grabbed the blanket throw from the back of the sofa, and draped it over me.

"Now, tell me what happened."

I don't know if it was her calm manner, or the unexpected care in her tone, but I immediately burst into tears.

CHAPTER
SEVEN

NANCY.

The tears didn't stop for a while. I cried and sobbed. My nose ran and my face was hot and red, and when Lexie shifted over to sit next to me, and offered me a shoulder, it didn't help put that stopper back on the bottle. I sobbed even harder.

But eventually I ran out of tears. I'd used half a box of tissues, and my sinuses were flowing.

"I'm a mess," I managed to get out.

Lexie just tucked her legs up under herself and pulled another blanket over her lap to stay warm. "You lost your dad, and you found out the guy you leaned on for love and support, didn't really love you. You're allowed to be devastated, Nancy."

The tears welled and fell but I didn't let it consume me again. "Thanks."

"I'll get you some water. I'll be right back." Lexie disappeared into the kitchen then came back with a woman's survival kit. A bottle of water, a block of chocolate, a tumbler glass, and an unopened bottle of whiskey.

"Which one do you want to start with?" she asked, chuckling.

My gaze fell over the things and I pointed tentatively to the whiskey. She popped open the bottle and sloshed some into the glass. "Good choice. Start with this." She handed it to me.

Then she ripped open the chocolate, cracked off a chunk for herself, and sat back down on the couch.

I threw back the whiskey, treating it like medicine and wincing as it burned my throat. "Ah... um, are you going to join me?"

She shook her head. "Nah, I'm all good."

She ate the chocolate, though, which was interesting. Was she pregnant? It wasn't really my place to ask, so I grabbed the bottle of water and rinsed the whiskey down.

"Okay. Go," she said. "Where the hell did you go?"

I gulped, feeling guilty as sin. "Um... the bus stop."

"You went to the bus stop?"

I nodded. "Yes. But I came back."

She narrowed her eyes. "How far did you get?"

"Ah... the main street."

Her eyes widened. "You mean you actually got on the bus?"

I nodded. "Yeah."

Lexie chuckled. "Those boys really freaked you out, didn't they?"

I nodded, wiping away new tears on my cheeks. I hadn't thought I had any left. "Um..."

"Look." Lexie clapped her hands together. "The boys wanted me to let you work all this stuff out for yourself, but I'm overruling them."

Heat flooded my face and body at the mention of the boys, and I pushed the blanket off my lap. "What do you mean?"

Lexie sighed. "You're freaked out by the poly thing, aren't you?"

I glanced away. "I'm not judging you; I mean, you seem really happy."

"You don't need to sugar coat it for me, don't worry. When Markus and Oliver told me they both wanted to date me, I almost died. I called them crazy among other things. But they won me over, and as you can see, I'm so happy its crazy to think that I ever thought they weren't for me. They're my world."

"But... isn't the brothers thing a bit weird?"

She cackled at that one and grabbed for the block of chocolate again. "Yeah, a little. When you think about it like everyone else does. But in their family, it's normal."

I blinked at her. "Sorry? What do you mean? They're all in poly groups?"

She sighed. "No, okay. So, in their family, when one of the women has a pair of unidentical twin boys, they call them perfect pairs. The boys are a perfect complement to each other. One of them is dark, the other light. One is funny and light hearted, the other more intense and serious. One governed more by their emotions and the other with a more intellectual bent. If you think about all the characteristics you might like in a man, they've got them. Only, across the both of them. Together, they make a perfect pair."

I finally reached for the chocolate, grabbing a square and sucking on it. "So you're saying they're like... a perfect man split into two?"

Lexie chuckled. "Sort of. Because really, the perfect man doesn't exist, does he? I mean, as a woman we want everything. We want a man who'll talk about his feelings and be a big mushy marshmallow, but then we want a man who'll be all alpha and take control in bed."

I chuckled, my throat aching from all the crying I'd done. "Yeah, you're right."

"So, you need to look past the fact that you think it's wrong to sleep with two men at once. And ignore the fact they're brothers, and just see if it feels right to you. Their focus will be on you, believe me."

I nodded, gulping at the swell of feelings that rose once more. That was the problem. It felt too natural, too amazing, to be with Tanner and Wade. To feel their adoration. To experience their amazing kisses on my lips. It was overwhelming, and I didn't fully understand why.

"Hey," I said, changing the topic before I had to admit anything too embarrassing. "I know this is gonna sound weird, but do you have wolves that come into town? I swear I saw two gray wolves just down the road, but you're quite a way from the forest here, aren't you? And... well, when they saw me they lay down. As if they knew I was scared and wanted to make me feel better."

Lexie had gone still; weirdly so.

"You okay?" I asked her.

"Um, yeah. We do have wolves in the area. But they're almost... well, they're not wild. Not really."

"What do you mean?" She couldn't be saying they were someone's pets, surely?

"Well... um, jeezus, I didn't want to be the one to tell you about that."

I frowned. "It's okay. I don't care, I was just wondering. It seemed weird to see them so close to people and housing, that's all."

Lexie hummed. "Yeah, well, table that as a conversation to have with your guys."

"My guys?" I repeated.

"Yeah. Tanner and Wade," Lexie said, totally serious.

I covered my face with my hands. "I can't believe you just said that."

"You mean you don't believe in soulmates, and you can't believe that two hot, sexy, amazing men would really want little old you?"

I dropped my hands and glared at her. "I'm not old."

Lexie chuckled. "Well, they are."

The anger that surged inside of me on their behalf was intense.

Lexie held up both of her hands. "Whoa. I didn't mean it like that."

I stood up and shook out my legs, just to give me something to do. "They're only what, thirty-five? Forty?"

I was angry, and my tone couldn't hide it.

"They're closer to forty, I think," Lexie said with a grin on her face. "Plenty old enough to know when they've found their soulmate."

"I don't believe in soulmates," I whispered, even though my gut was calling me a liar.

Lexie grinned and stood up. "Look, I know we just met but if you'll trust me, I won't steer you wrong. Those two men will be the best thing that ever happens to you, I can almost guarantee it. The only thing that's gonna stop you guys being happy, is you."

"Me?" I gasped out.

"Yes. If you let your worries or insecurities or old-fashioned thinking get in your way."

I opened my mouth to respond, with absolutely no idea what I was going to say. After a moment, I snapped my mouth shut again.

Lexie was already heading for the stairs. "I've gotta get back to bed. The boys get up super early and they'll be losing sleep without me there with them. See you in the morning."

My host waved and headed up the stairs once more.

I stared after her. What a night! I poured myself another splash of whiskey, knocked it back, then walked up the stairs to my lovely bedroom.

The sheets were cool, but the room was dark and I felt safe. I thought it would take forever to fall asleep but when I closed my eyes I drifted off quickly and got the most restful night's sleep I'd had since my father died.

Nancy.

When I woke in the morning I stretched my arms above my head and exulted in the warmth and comfort of the bed cradling me.

For the past six nights, I'd barely slept. I would arrive late into a town and either pay to stay in a crappy motel, or find a safe place to put my head down for an hour.

I didn't know what time it was, but there was bright sunshine outlined around the curtains and I needed to pee. I threw back the covers and climbed out of the king-sized bed, then tiptoed to the bathroom I'd used yesterday.

The house was quiet and felt empty. I made my way down the

stairs and into the kitchen to find a note on the counter, with a silver key sticky-taped to the paper.

Morning Nancy,

We've all gone to work, but I've left a stack of clean clothes on the couch for you and help yourself to anything in the fridge.

Here's a house key in case you want to go for a walk, but otherwise, see you after work.

Lex, Markus and Ollie.

I smiled down at the note, getting a warm and fuzzy feeling. Lexie had to be younger than me, and yet she was mothering me.

It had been a long time since anyone had looked after me in such a way.

My stomach churned and I wandered over to the fridge and pulled out a bottle of fresh orange juice. I couldn't stop thinking about Wade and Tanner, even though I tried to focus on my breakfast. Yoghurt. Fruit.

Don't think about them. My guys, Lexie had called them.

I couldn't get rid of the feeling that I was exactly where I needed to be. I was filled with relief, and light, even though I knew Travis and his men would be looking for me.

Maybe. They didn't know what direction I'd ridden in. Was it possible that they hadn't crossed two state lines to find me?

I walked over to the window that looked out on the yard and stared at the grass and the flowered garden beds. Lexie and her men had gone full-on suburban family with this place. Two sexy guys and a curvy girl. Who would have thought it?

Was it possible for me too? Was there something in the water out here that made gorgeous twins love women like me? It seemed so ridiculous. But the proof was in front of me. In this house. With this family. Lexie really was loved and cherished by her men.

I wandered to the foyer and looked out the front window beside the door. No-one knew me here. If I wore Lexie's clothes and tied up my hair, Travis and his men might not find me even if they did roll into town.

I cleaned up the kitchen, grabbed the house key and changed into the fresh clothes Lexie had left for me. The bike shop wasn't far and I wanted to check in with Toni. So, I grabbed my phone and wallet and headed out the door, locking the house behind me.

Going for a walk couldn't get me into too much trouble, surely?

My brother wasn't in a good way. He was antsy as hell and in a bit of a mood.

"Did you sleep at all last night?" I asked Wade over breakfast, pouring myself a cup of coffee.

Wade shrugged and grunted as he shoveled in some crunchy granola.

"Yeah, that's what I thought." I sat down and took a sip of the caffeinated bitterness. "What do you think about buying another place? Something bigger."

I glanced around our outdated two-bedroom unit. It was close to our parents' house, and had suited us for a while, but we had money piling up in our bank account and our fated mate was now on the horizon. We needed to be ready, in case Nancy came around to the idea of the two of us loving her.

No, not if, I told myself. When.

Wade glanced up, then shrugged again. "Yeah. If you want."

That was it? "Really?"

"Yeah. Sure. If you wanna spend more time in town, we'll need something closer to the forest. Something bigger."

The run through the forest last night was amazing. To stretch inside my wolf body and howl at the crescent moon. My shifter was aching for more.

"Cool."

I cleaned up and grabbed my cell phone, glancing down at the screen, again.

"She doesn't even have our numbers," Wade said, "Stop looking at your cell."

"You don't think Lexie would have passed our numbers on?"

"Nope."

I grabbed the truck keys. "You coming?"

Wade turned to me, his eyebrows lowered. "Where you going?"

"Gonna do a drive by, maybe see Nancy."

Wade stood up and pulled his T-shirt off over his head. "Enjoy. I'm off to shower."

Then he walked away.

I called after him. "Don't be a soft cock, Wade."

My brother gave me the finger and didn't even turn around.

I shrugged and headed out the door. Wade might be angry and hurt, and acting like a fucking pussy, but I was excited. We'd found our mate, after so many years, and she was here. In our town. She was single and in need of love, affection and safety.

That was fine by me. I had love to give. Plenty of it. We had money. We had time.

Hell, if she wanted us to live in our truck next to her uncle's house until she was ready to speak to us, I'd do it. And I knew Wade would, too. Though he'd be seething while he did it.

We had a goal, and a destination. Nancy would be ours, because the fates had pre-ordained it. I just had to remind myself to be patient. We needed to seduce her into giving us a chance, because surely once she got to know us, things would develop naturally.

I climbed into my truck and drove down the street to where Ollie and Markus lived with Lexie. The house seemed empty. Maybe Nancy had gone out too?

I turned the truck around and headed toward Toni's shop, intending to chat to Lexie and see if she knew where Nancy was. A lot of our family rode bikes and although Wade and I had dabbled as kids, we didn't own a motor bike.

Maybe it was time we changed that? Nancy certainly seemed to enjoy riding. Maybe we could make it a family event or tradition.

When I pulled up next to Toni's shop I could immediately feel my mate. My senses prickled and it felt like I came properly alive.

I jumped out and locked up, hurrying into the mechanic's workshop. Toni was there, working on Nancy's pink Harley. "Hey Toni."

"Tanner." She hopped to her feet. "What can I do for you today?"

"I'm actually looking for..."

Nancy walked around the corner, freezing the moment she saw me. "Ah... hi."

"Hey." I grinned at her. "I was just coming to see if you want to go out for lunch."

Lexie stepped into the mechanic space from the office. "That's a great idea."

"I just came to check on my bike," Nancy said in a rush.

"It's going well," Toni said, wiping her hands on a rag. "I ordered the parts we needed yesterday and I'm doing some rebuilding now."

"But I haven't paid for anything." Nancy sounded panicked.

Toni shrugged. "It's all good. We'll sort everything out. Go have lunch with Tanner."

Nancy gaped at Toni, then me. "But..."

I walked toward her and smiled, trying to appear non-threatening. "Come on. You don't wanna argue with Toni."

I led the way outside and Nancy followed, though slowly. I grinned back at her, loving how my wolf practically made a jig inside my mind. He was so happy to finally have his mate around. He was much more patient than Wade's wolf and I knew we could take it slow—if that's what she needed from us. "Come on."

Nancy hurried a little, catching up with me. "I'm not dressed to go out anywhere."

I let my gaze peruse her body, from head to toe. "You look good enough to eat, but hey, if you need to do some shopping, I wouldn't say no to showing you around town."

She blinked owlishly at me. "Sorry?"

I shoved my hands in my pockets, so I didn't reach out and grab her. "We've got two little sisters, and lots of female cousins. I can show you where the good shops are. In fact..." I stopped and nodded toward Little M's. "There's one, over there. I'll show you."

"Oh, I'm traveling light. I don't really need any other clothes."

I placed my hands in the small of her back and guided her forward. "Come on. I want to introduce you to someone."

Nancy allowed my guidance and pushed open the door to the women's clothing shop in front of us.

"Oh, it's a bit funky for me," she whispered.

I laughed, glancing around at the latest decorations that Madelyn had thrown around the shop. "She does have a rather colorful style, doesn't she?'

"Who?" Nancy asked, her tone curious.

"Tanner!" Madelyn hollered, rushing up to jump into my arms.

I hugged her tightly. "Hey Maddi."

When I put her down, Nancy's face was on fire and her eyes spat anger. I couldn't help but laugh a little, even though her glare would have felled a lesser man. I put her out of her misery as quickly as I could. "Nancy, this is my baby sister, Madelyn."

The anger left Nancy's gaze and her shoulders visibly dropped. "Oh! I'm sorry..."

"For what?' Maddi said.

"Oh... ah..."

I elbowed my sister in the side. "She thought you might be my lover; I think."

"Eww!" Maddie screwed up her face and Nancy's cheeks immediately turned even more red.

I knew it! The fact that she was instantly jealous was a good sign. It meant she felt something for me, too.

"Anyway, Maddi, this is Nancy. Her bike broke down as she was passing through town and had nothing to wear. Can you get her a couple of outfits to try?"

Maddi's face lit up. "Of course! What's your style? What colors do you like?"

I pulled Maddi in and whispered at a level only a wolf shifter could hear. "Don't let her pay for anything. I'll cover it. I'll explain later."

Maddi's eyes twinkled. She likely assumed Nancy was just a woman of mine, so it was lovely of her to be so nice. But once she heard that Nancy was my mate, then she was going to throw a bloody party. I didn't want that intensity on Nancy. Not yet.

"Oh, no, I..." Nancy was trying to stop my sister from rushing her to the change rooms, but she was in a losing battle.

"Don't fight it," I called out to Nancy from the door. "You don't really stand a chance."

"Oh, shut up big brother," Maddi waved her hand at me. "Go sit in the husband chairs and we'll be out soon."

I did what my little sister said, because we all did. I found the corner of Maddi's shop where she'd set up a little husband haven. Two couches, a mini fridge with beer and a small TV with the sports channel on mute.

I sat but didn't drink or watch sports. I looked around the shop and marveled at what my little sister had done over the last few years.

When Maddi came out again, she waved her hands around as though she were putting on a presentation, or something. "Check her out."

Nancy crept out, not with a swagger or cat walk confidence, but like someone who'd never been dressed by a professional stylist before. She tugged at the long black top and hunched her shoulders. "I'm not sure about the color."

The leggings were black also and although part of me understood when Maddi thought Nancy was an all-dark-colors chick, I knew better.

"Nancy's bike is metallic pink, if that helps, Maddi?"

Maddi's jaw dropped and she turned to Nancy. "Seriously?"

Nancy's smile was as sweet as pie. "I do like color."

Maddi squealed. "Oh my God, that is so much more fun. Come, come, come." She waved her hands around and started grabbing up things. "I wish I had big boobs like yours. You're gonna love this top!"

I saw Nancy's grimace but I didn't say anything because I wanted to see what outfit Maddi was going to put her in next.

When Nancy emerged, my stomach twisted, and I staggered to my feet. "Wow."

She tucked her long dark hair behind her ear. "It's a bit much."

Tight blue jeans wrapped her luscious legs, a black tank had a low V-neck that exposed her voluptuous breasts, and a bright pink cardigan topped the outfit off.

"You look amazing," I managed, my fingers tingling to touch her. "That top... the jeans, they're great."

Nancy flashed my sister a smile. "You've got a great eye for style. I don't normally find clothes that fit my body."

Maddi waved a hand. "Oh, you've got a great body. I've got so much that will fit you."

"Oh, no. Just this outfit please."

"Well, it's on the house," Maddi said. "Welcome to town."

"Oh, you can't do that."

The shop door opened, and Maddi waved at us. "I can, and I have. Time to work. Bye, brother!"

Nancy's eyes were shimmering. "I don't know what to say."

This time I did reach out and touch her. I couldn't help it. I cupped her face and stared down into her emotional eyes. "You say thank you, then you grab those other clothes to give back to Lexie, and we go have some lunch. How about that?"

Maddi walked over with a pair of ankle high black boots. "Here you go. I guessed... size thirty-four?"

Nancy nodded. "But I can't."

Maddi rolled her eyes. "Here. Take. Nice meeting you."

I grinned at Nancy. "Put 'em on and we can go."

Nancy nodded and headed to the changing rooms. "I'll be right back."

I let her go only because I loved watching her leave.

NINE

NANCY.

I sat down to pull the black boots on my feet. They were soft and had great arch support. I'd never owned such an amazing pair of casual shoes.

I stood up and had a look in the mirror. "Oh my God!" I whispered the words because I didn't want anyone to rush in and think I'd fallen and couldn't get up.

The woman looking back at me in from the mirror was beautiful, in a way I'd never been able to see myself. Until now.

Before I got too swept up in how overwhelmed I was, I grabbed up Lexie's clothes and walked out into the shop. Tanner, the gorgeous blond Viking, was waiting for me by the door.

His smile was wide, and it filled my tummy with butterflies. "Come on, beautiful." He called, holding out his hand to me.

I took his hand and let him walk outside with me. The sun was shining and when I stumbled on a bit of uneven concrete, one of Tanner's arms came around me and held me safe and tight.

"Thanks," I said, when it was time to step back and continue our walk, but something had changed between us. I wasn't sure what it was. But it felt good. "Where do you want to go and eat?"

He shrugged. "Anywhere, really. As long as I'm with you."

I inhaled sharply and looked around. I didn't really like it when he said stuff like that. It was super embarrassing.

"How about Grayson's?" Tanner said. "They're a classic diner and their burgers are great."

"Sure," I said. Couldn't go wrong with a diner. Surely?

"Hey Tanner!" A guy walked up and smiled at us.

Tanner's hand went around my waist and tugged me into his side in a possessive move I couldn't help but recognize. And neither could the other guy. His eyebrows rose a little. "Hello." The newcomer had orange-red hair and beautiful blue eyes, but he didn't hold a candle to my two guys.

My two guys? Oh, hell.

"Hey," I managed, then looked up at Tanner, waiting for an introduction.

He didn't speak.

"You okay, Tanner?" the red-haired guy asked, frowning at him.

Tanner nodded but didn't say anything.

It was awkward-as so I decided to step up and help the two guys out. "Well, I'm starving. So, let's keep going. Bye." I tugged at my blond giant and managed to drag him down the street toward the diner he'd mentioned.

By the time we got to Grayson's diner, Tanner had relaxed and was speaking again.

"Sorry about that."

"What happened?" I asked. "Is that an old enemy or something?"

Tanner laughed. "Actually, no. He's a pack mate. We get along well."

"A pack mate?" I repeated. What the hell was that?

Tanner gulped and I swear his cheeks darkened slightly. "Ah... here we go. Let's get a table." He opened the door to the diner and effectively dodged the question.

By the time we sat down, ordered our food and received our

drinks, I was ready to quiz him. "Tell me what you meant about that pack reference?"

Wolves were in packs, right? Lexie had hinted that there was something weird about the wolves in this area. Did Tanner own some pet wolves? Maybe the red-haired guy owned some, too?

"Oh, it's nothing," Tanner said, staring down at the menu, even though we'd already ordered.

I sighed, deciding to bluff. "Well, Lexie told me that there's something special about you guys and the wolves. This whole town is surrounded by them."

Tanner's gaze came up and met mine. "She told you?"

"Yep." I nodded.

"And you're okay with it?" He sounded shocked.

I shrugged. "Yeah. Of course. The wolves aren't dangerous, right?" I had no idea if I was going down the right path, but this sounded important.

His smile was as brilliant as the sun. "That's bloody brilliant. I'm so relieved. We didn't think you'd accept us if you knew the truth."

The truth? "About the wolves? Are you saying they're dangerous?"

"No. Of course not. We're in full control when we're in wolf form."

I gulped the orange juice in my throat, coughing as the liquid got stuck. Wolf form.

"When you're in wolf form?" I repeated.

"Yes," Tanner said, then blinked. "You said she told you about us."

My heart beat harder. Wolf form. Wolf... form. They... turned into wolves?

I shook my head because it made no sense, but I couldn't shake the question away. "I saw two wolves last night, on Lexie's Street. They... lay down and looked at me. As if they wanted to make me feel safe."

Tanner leaned back in his seat and picked up his knife and fork as the waitress placed a stack of pancakes in front of him.

When she walked away to fetch my order, he raised an eyebrow. "Lexie didn't tell you about us, did she?"

I pressed my lips together, so a frightened laugh didn't escape. "No. Well... she told me that there was something special about the wolves and you guys, but that I should hear it from you. So, since you've told me a bit, can you tell me the whole lot?"

I was talking too much, my brain pulling up all the little bits of information I'd picked up on and dragging it all together.

The pack. Fated Mates. Wolf form.

It was all slotting together like an unbelievable puzzle that my brain refused to accept.

"You promise you're not going to run out of here screaming?" Tanner asked, cutting his pancakes into pieces but not eating anything yet.

"I... can't promise that until I know what you're going to tell me."

The waitress put my beef and bacon burger down in front of me and I put both hands on the table, trying not to get up and run.

Running was kinda my thing.

"Okay," Tanner said, leaning forward and whispering. "We're wolf shifters, not werewolves or anything. We don't bite. It's not an infection that spreads. And we have full control of our shifter bodies, so you never have to worry about us."

I was totally shocked, and yet, the world kept spinning. Around and around us. People were talking and walking, and yet, my world had stopped.

I swallowed hard, then attempted to talk. When no words came out, I took a sip of my juice again and said, "So, you... and Wade. Last night."

"Yes, that was us. My brother and I went for a run after you threw us out. We were pretty upset and thought running in the forest would release some of our tension. Why were you out walking?"

I stared down at my burger. "I... ah, almost got on a bus and left town."

Tanner's knife clattered loudly, and I winced as he scooped up the cutlery. He'd dropped it onto his plate. "Sorry. I... you... You were planning to leave?"

The expression on his face was so devastated I rushed to reassure him. "I know, I'm sorry. But I came straight back. It felt so wrong to leave I almost threw up. I'm just... scared."

"Why?" Tanner demanded. "Because we want you so much? Because we've waited our whole lives for you?"

I stared down at my plate once more. I really couldn't cope with that sort of guilt. I didn't know anything about them.

"I didn't know that." I lifted my head and stared into his hurt eyes. "So don't say shit like that to me. So what, you've been waiting for me, have you?"

"Yes." He hissed back. "For years. Decades. Our whole lives."

"Where the hell were you, huh?" I growled back. "When I was lonely, and sad, and so depressed I would have killed myself if it wasn't for my dad. Where were you when Travis was taking advantage of my grief? Well?"

Tanner pushed back, his eyes widening with pain. "We didn't know where you were."

"Well, I didn't know where you were!" I practically screamed at him. "I didn't know there were men, two states away, who wanted me. Who'd look after me. Who'd treat me like... like..."

"Like what?" Tanner countered. "Like the goddess you are? Like the perfect woman you are?"

"I'm not perfect." My voice had dropped to a whisper.

"You're perfect for us," he said. "A perfect woman for a perfect pair. That's how it works."

A tear slipped down my cheek, "I'm scared."

Tanner reached out for me, but I was too far away. He stood, reached for my hands, and tugged me to my feet.

"What are you doing?" I asked, glancing around at all the eyes on us. "Everyone is looking."

He cupped his big, strong hands around my jaw and stared into my eyes. His eyes were so blue, and beautiful, and I still couldn't believe a man this gorgeous wanted a woman like me.

"Good. Let them watch and know that you're mine and I'm yours."

Before I could debate that supposed fact, his lips met mine. His kiss wasn't just a kiss. It was an oath, a promise. And as my eyes closed and I gripped his shirt to haul him closer, my heart called out in response. Yes!

When Tanner finally lifted his head, a roar of laughter and applause went up around us.

I buried my head against his chest.

"Hey, can we get our food to go?" Tanner asked someone nearby, and I smiled and kept my eyes closed.

"Let's go, beautiful." I nodded and ran, but this time, I was headed in the same direction as my man.

TEN

After a long shower I went downstairs and made some lunch. I wasn't going to help Tanner go find Nancy. I refused to run after her like some little lap dog. But God, I wanted to. I needed my mate, but she obviously didn't need us. I grabbed a beer from the fridge and popped it open. Damn, life sucked sometimes. Just when I'd thought things were changing, that we were set for the life we deserved, we were screwed over, again.

The back door opened, and I turned to greet whoever was walking into our home. It could only be my parents, or Tanner. They were the only ones with a key.

"Hey," I nodded to my brother as he wandered in, grinning like a kook. "What…"

And then I saw her, right behind my brother. Our mate. "Nancy?"

My heart began to thud. What was going on?

She smiled in greeting, her lips red and softly swollen. "Hi Wade."

"How did you…" I walked forward to grab hold of her hands, aware that I was probably crowding her but so grateful that she was back that I couldn't contain my need to touch her.

"Tanner found me and we had a chat," she said. "I'm still not sure about this whole wolf thing. But at this point in my life I figure, if you aren't going to hit me, gamble away my money or demean me for being fat, I'm willing to try anything."

I could tell she was kinda joking since her eyes sparkled with mischief, but there was a serious undertone I couldn't ignore. "I'm not sure what Tanner's explained, but we want you as ours forever. We'd never hit you, never cheat on you, and our money is all yours. You will always be our number one priority, Nancy. We would cherish you, not hurt you."

Her gaze dimmed a little but the happiness I'd felt when she first entered was still pulsing through her. "Well, that's... ah..."

"Overwhelming, as usual, Wade." Tanner crossed his arms over his chest and glared at me.

I slid a hand around my mate's waist. "I was just being honest."

Nancy didn't move away but seemed a little awkward. "Um... so, this is your place?"

Tanner reached out his hand and tugged her out of my arms. "Yeah, come. We'll give you the short tour. This is the kitchen and eating area, obviously. And through here is the living area."

I followed behind my brother, feeling a little left out of the conversation. What had they talked about this morning? What had I missed?

And did I really need to know? It was obvious she'd had a big turnaround in her attitude toward us.

"Our bedrooms are through there and there's one bathroom." Tanner was pointing and explaining. "It's pretty small and simple but has suited us for the past decade."

She was nodding and making all the right noises, but I knew there was nothing impressive about our accommodation.

"We've been waiting for our mate," I said, and she turned to stare at me with her big, beautiful eyes. "There was no point buying a big family house when it was just us."

"You always knew you were going to share a wife... or partner, or whatever?" She wandered around the room, though there wasn't much to look at.

"It wasn't guaranteed…" Tanner said.

"But it was pretty likely," I added. "Most perfect pairs share a mate."

"A mate," Nancy repeated. "A… fated mate. That's a wolf thing, yeah?"

I glanced across at Tanner, who was leaning against the doorway as though he was holding up the wall. He smiled at me and once again I felt at sea without a clue.

I coughed to clear my throat. "Yeah… how much do you know about that?"

"She saw us last night," Tanner said. "Under the street light."

I stared at her. "And you're okay about it?"

She chuckled, then shrugged her shoulders. "No… I have no idea how I feel about that. But at the moment I'm kinda ignoring it and… hang on a second. Are Lexie's guys, you know?"

I nodded. "Yep. Toni too."

"The mechanic?" Nancy gaped at me, then chuckled. "Girl wolf… people."

"Wolf shifters," I corrected.

She stared at me for a moment in that assessing way she had, then nodded. "So, you've found me and now you'll just what? Buy a big house and start a big poly family with me, like Lexie?"

I frowned at her. "Is this a trick question?"

She burst out laughing, running her hands through her hair. "Oh my God, this is just… crazy."

"It's not crazy," I growled at her. "Crazy is going insane night after night dreaming about the moment you'll meet the woman who will complete you, then finding out she's running from a man who hurt her and might be too afraid to ever accept the two men who actually love her."

The next growl that rolled out of my throat was menacing; even I could hear the tone. "I'll fucking kill him if he hurts you."

Nancy stumbled toward me as though she couldn't stop herself. "You... you want to protect me? You would do that for me? You don't even know me."

I met her in the middle of the lounge room, where she seemed to be having trouble standing.

When I grabbed her around the waist to hold her steady, the tingle of awareness that passed between us was warm. Not shocking, not painful. A deep knowing; a thrill.

"Hmm... I'm still not used to that," I said, my growling tone turning soft. She felt so damn good in my arms.

I dropped my head to kiss her lightly on the lips. She didn't flinch away. In fact, she lifted her chin to meet my caress with her own. Her fingers dug into my arms, tight. As though she never wanted me to let go.

"You know the only way to know if we truly are meant to be?"

She lifted her chin higher and whispered against my lips, "No. What?"

"Sex," I whispered back. "When we enter you, join our bodies with yours... you'll know as surely as we already do."

A sob rose in her throat and before I could ask her if I'd said something wrong she groaned out, "Promise?"

I crushed her to me, kissing her hard. She wrapped her arms around my neck and pressed her soft breasts against my chest.

The groan that rolled through me this time was soul deep and born of pure need. I squeezed my arms around her and kissed her deeper, thrusting my tongue between her open lips to taste her. God, she was even sweeter than I'd ever imagined my mate would be.

My hands slid down to her huge ass, grabbing a big handful and squeezing hard. I'd never been with a woman with a body like hers and had often wondered what drew a man to a woman who wasn't classically thin.

But my God! She was heavenly. I couldn't wait to rest my head on her breasts and feel her skin against mine as we slept.

When she pulled away from me, her chest was heaving. Tanner

tugged her toward him and, as he grabbed her face and kissed her deep, my cock made a play to grab my brain's attention. He wanted to sink into her body and cum hard.

I coughed and got the attention of both of them. My cock was straining against my jeans, and I popped the button and let down the zipper, unable to hold back any longer. Nancy's gaze dropped straight to my groin and her eyes widened.

"Bed time?" I raised my eyebrows.

She glanced up at Tanner, then back at me, and her brows furrowed. "You sleep together already?"

That made me laugh and nicely defused the sudden tension in the room from my bold action. "Hell no. He snores like a train."

"Pot, kettle, much?" Tanner said.

I grinned at him, then turned my attention back to our mate. "No, love. We've slept in separate beds our whole life, but once you join us, we'll never sleep apart again. You are our focus, one hundred percent. So, if the question is, which bedroom right now? My bed's bigger."

Nancy inhaled deeply, her body shuddering as though she were on the brink of turning away.

My heart rocketed. Had I pushed her too fast? "Hey, if you don't want to..." I wasn't sure how I'd handle her rejection at this point, but if she didn't want this, I'd have to. I'd be damned if I ever forced a woman. Ever.

She gazed at me with so much confused lust I played one of the only cards I had. My body.

I reached up pulled off my T-shirt, moving slowly to give her time to take in the view. Then shucked down the jeans that already sat around my hips unzipped and ready to fall.

Nancy's gaze raked me up and down before settling on my cock, which was hard and ready.

"And if you dare think I don't want you, then I'm sorry... but I'd say you're wrong."

She wet her lips with the tip of her tongue before walking forward and dropping to her knees.

I stared down at her, unable to believe that this was actually happening. When she looked up from her place of prayer, eyes wide and desire written all over her features, I slid my fingers into her hair, deciding that if this was a dream, I must have died and gone to heaven.

ELEVEN

NANCY.

I closed down that part of my brain that was scared or insecure. It felt so right to be here now, with Wade naked in front of me and Tanner nearby. I wanted to feel loved, secure and protected. I wanted to worship this man's body and hope that in turn, he'd do the same to me.

I wrapped my hand around Wade's cock, loving the thick heat of him. I'd never been one to enjoy this, but my God, my mouth was watering at the sight of his one-eyed monster so large and seemingly ready. Because of me.

When I opened my mouth and took the head of his cock between my lips, he didn't drive it home or try to conquer me. In fact, he gently patted my hair and stroked my face without moving my mouth at all.

I took my time exploring his length. His taste. My body reacted in an amazing way, pleasure tugging at my core. I loved his patience, but part of me craved him taking over now. But I was too shy to ask for that.

Wade pulled back out of my grasp, and hauled me to my feet. My disappointment was immense. But then he groaned and said,

"Damn girl. If you keep doing that I'm going to cum before we even begin. Let's get to bed."

When I turned around Tanner was also naked, having undressed while I was on my knees. I had the urge to drop down again. Tanner was taller, bigger, even more muscled. "Oh my God."

Tanner chuckled at my reaction and walked toward me, reaching for my cardigan and slowly peeling it off my shoulders. "That was my first thought when I saw you, beautiful girl."

Was this for real? These two guys both seemed to be hot for me. I couldn't quite believe it and yet, here they were. Proving me wrong with their obvious erections, their gentle hands and their desire-filled eyes.

Between them, the boys stripped all my clothes off until I was down to my panties. I held my boobs up and covered them with my arms, and twisted my legs so they couldn't strip me completely. "Can we go somewhere darker?"

I did not want them to see my ass in the stark light of day. My thighs were dimpled and yuck. My stomach...

"Come this way," Tanner said, leading me toward a bedroom door and pushing it open.

Neither of them tried to pull my arms down, but instead, Wade put a hand on my lower back and gently pushed me into the bedroom.

I was shocked to see how big the space was. The bed was a king and the furniture was lovely—masculine and heavy in design and color, but still beautiful.

Tanner drew the curtains and flicked on a lamp beside the bed. "I'm keeping it dark for you, but just so you know, we'd rather see you in bright daylight."

I chuckled. "Thanks. But this is much more flattering."

Wade moved around behind me, fitting his naked cock against my back and one of his hands sliding under my crossed arms.

"Let me touch you." He whispered enticing words into my ear. I dropped my arms so he could slide his hand up and cup one of my breasts.

I threw my head back against his shoulder and moaned as he stroked my flesh and rubbed his fingertips over my nipples. First one, then the other. He gave them equal attention and every touch added to my growing need.

Tanner walked up in front of me and dropped to his knees, grabbing the sides of my panties and pulling them down. With Wade working my breasts, my resistance slipped away. I stepped out of my last piece of armor. I was naked, and they could see me.

All of me.

My belly... my thighs...

"Damn, you're beautiful." Tanner groaned, then leaned forward and stuck his tongue between my thighs.

I gasped and recoiled, jumping out of both of their grips and bolting over to the bed. I was not used to that sort of attention. "Um... go slow. Okay?"

They nodded and Tanner got to his feet, prowling toward me like the predatory animals they admitted they were.

Calm down. Let go.

I sat down on the edge of the bed and shimmied back. Maybe I could just lie on my back and they'd jump on top of me? They both certainly looked ready.

"Lie here, if you can." Tanner said, patting the edge of the bed.

I nodded and moved into the position he wanted. I wasn't sure why exactly until Tanner stood beside my head and grabbed his cock to feed it to me.

I opened my lips and took him in, and at the same time, Wade's hands were on my thighs, opening my legs. I closed my eyes and focused on Tanner's cock, until Wade's kisses started moving up my thighs.

My legs convulsed, tightening and closing around his head.

"Open for me," Wade said, and although his tone was gentle, his hands were not. He pushed at my thighs to get me to open up again. "I want to get you ready for us."

I lifted my head. "I'm already ready. You don't have to do that."

"Oh, but I need to do it," Wade said with an intent look. "Turn-about's fair play, surely?"

I groaned in anticipation and lay back, loosening my legs for Wade's probing touch. I wasn't sure what I expected, but from the moment I sucked Tanner's cock back into my mouth, pleasure hit me from all directions. Tanner worked on my breasts with his fingers while gently fucking my face. Wade's tongue did wondrous things to my body, flicking my clit over and over again and dipping into and along my seam.

Pleasure I'd never experienced before washed over me, with every kiss. Every touch. They pushed my pleasure higher and higher, making me ache and gasp at a level I'd never felt before.

"Oh, fuckkk..." I groaned around Tanner's cock.

My belly was so tight, shuddering with every step closer to orgasm.

"She's ready," Tanner said, withdrawing his cock from my mouth and stepping back.

"Where do you want me?" I asked, sitting up.

"Head on the pillow for me, beautiful," Tanner said, and I scrabbled up to lie where he said.

He crawled over the top of me, and I opened my legs to welcome him. He didn't wait long. He set his cock at my entrance and then slid inside of me with one long thrust.

"Oh... ah..." I arched my back to try and accommodate him. He was stretching me, filling me, and the ache of lonely need inside my belly finally began to subside.

He set his hands on either side of me and pushed up to give me space, then dropped his head to kiss my lips. I cupped his face and stroked my tongue against his while I lifted my thighs to draw him deeper into my body.

He groaned into my mouth and began to move, drawing back, then gently thrusting forward.

The ache inside of me flared again, only this time it turned into something else. Something more terrifying. A growing hunger that felt insatiable. As if I could never get enough of this beautiful man inside me.

I moved my hands over his skin, loving the feel of his chest, his arms. The huge muscles beneath his flesh. He moved faster and I began to moan at the pleasure that rushed through me. And gasp and cry out as I reached the edge of my precipice.

Tanner fucked me harder, pushing me over the edge and into the bliss. I swallowed my scream as white light exploded inside my head. My belly convulsed as my pussy squeezed his cock, milking his shaft.

Tanner's release triggered and with an almighty groan, he thrust deep inside my body and came. His pulsing heat made me come again, another pleasure wave hitting me.

This time I did scream, unable to hold the feelings inside. The pleasure was too intense, too perfect, and that's when I knew. This man had been telling me the truth. I was meant for them, as they were for me.

Somehow, I had managed to find my mates.

Tanner rolled us to the side, still inside of me, his smile dazzling. "Wow. That was..."

I nodded, still trying to catch my breath. "I know."

My gaze caught on Wade's solemn face. He was still standing by the bed, still ready for me. His eyes blazed with unspoken need and I realized the extraordinary experience wasn't over yet.

I glanced at Tanner, who nodded and gently withdrew before rolling away.

I sat up and slid over to the edge of the bed where Wade stood. "Are you okay?"

He nodded but didn't speak.

I bit my lip. "Um."

"Roll over." He groaned out the words and I could have sworn his teeth were different. Sharper. "Ass up."

I didn't think. I rolled over, knelt on the bed and spread my legs for him. Somehow, even with two orgasms and the best sex of my life with Tanner, I wasn't fully satisfied.

Wade's hand on my back had me dropping my head down and tilting my back to give him easier access to me.

He set the head of his cock at my entrance, slid both of his hands around my hips to grab tight, then pulled me back into him. His cock impaled me with one sharp thrust, but instead of any pain, it was all bliss.

Wade didn't start slow; he fucked me deep and hard, and steady. His rhythm was intoxicating, pushing me higher and higher up the hill of pleasure.

I met him with each thrust, letting myself moan and groan as the feelings rolled through my belly. And when his movements became erratic, faster and faster, I let myself fly.

I came so hard, biting into the bedcovers as I shuddered and shook with release. Wade followed me only seconds later, roaring into the silence and filling me with his heat.

I collapsed forward, rolling into a ball as convulsions continued to wrack my body. But I wasn't alone. Wade was there, spooning me, holding me, kissing my neck and telling me how amazing I was.

And that's when I started to cry, because what could be more heartbreaking than meeting the perfect men at the worst time of your life?

TWELVE

WADE.

"Oh, baby girl, what's wrong? Did I hurt you?" I cuddled Nancy while she was wracked with sobs.

If I'd caused these tears by hurting her, I'd cut my own heart out.

"No. No. It's not you." She managed to speak between each gasped-out cry.

"Come on," Tanner said to her. "Hop under the covers and lie with us." He pulled back the covers and I managed to scoop her up and put her beneath the sheets.

Then we climbed under the covers too, one each side of Nancy. Tanner positioned Nancy's head on his chest, and I stroked her back, staying close. I didn't like going second, after Tanner. He was the firstborn twin, the confident, suave and happy one of the two of us.

And when he'd made love to Nancy first, I'd been filled with envy, then love for the joy Nancy got from their encounter, then disappointment that it hadn't been me. But as soon as she slid over to me and looked up with those eyes that were only for me, all the negative feelings fell away to reveal a wolf shifter desperate for his mate.

I didn't really want to share her with my brother, but Fate had decreed that we had to. I'd do anything to keep her safe and happy, and if that meant she needed Tanner as much as me, then that's what would happen.

Her happiness was paramount. I dipped my fingers into her hair, playing with the strands, hoping our touch would soothe her.

Tanner found a Kleenex box from the bedside table and grabbed a few for Nancy to cry into. When she was finally done, she blew her nose, mopped her face, then excused herself to use the bathroom.

She slid out from between us and we were left alone, together.

"Well.... Ah..." I sat up with my back against the headboard and looked at Tanner. "Do you know what that was about?"

He slid further down under the covers, but stayed as far away from me as he could get. "Don't ask me. I've never made anyone cry before."

I had, once or twice. But only because the women's orgasms had been so intense. They'd laughed as they cried. Not the way Nancy had sobbed, like her heart was broken.

"I..." Nancy stepped back into the room, a towel wrapped around her.

"Do you want a night shirt or something?" I asked, jumping from the bed to grab a flannel shirt out of my collection.

"Thanks," she said, walking up to take it, then turning her back to slide the shirt on.

I stared at her back and almost smirked at the action. Turning away now seemed a bit like the proverbial shutting the door once the horse had bolted, but whatever she needed was fine by me.

But I couldn't stop myself from adding, "Covered all your beauty up now?"

She shrugged and rushed back to the safety of the blankets, and our bed. I stared after her, glanced at my brother, then joined her again in bed. This time she cuddled onto my chest, and it was Tanner who was left to cuddle her ass, not that 'getting the ass' in her case was a bad thing. It was so delectably sexy.

"So..." She spoke slowly, tapping her fingers along my breastbone and not quite meeting my eyes. "About this wolf thing. Were you, like, joking? Do you have pet wolves in the backyard or something?"

I sighed. "No. We weren't joking."

Tanner slid away from Nancy and rolled out of the bed on the other side to me. "Do you wanna see one of us shift?"

She sat up and stared at my brother as he stood naked at the foot of the bed. "Do I have to?"

I sat up and put an arm around her. "Of course, you don't have to. But it is a large part of who we are. We've heard that humans can freak out a bit about this part, but we've never shown anyone before. We only want to show you because, well, you're our mate."

She looked up at me, her eyes round and shiny. "You're serious, aren't you?"

I exhaled slowly, then kissed her, hard. "Yes. Now let's just get this part over and done with. Do you need a whiskey or something?"

She shook her hands out in front of her and took a deep breath. "No. Remind of the things. The good things."

What the hell were the good things? "Um... Well, when Tanner shifts, it'll be just for a minute, and then he'll shift right back, okay?"

"And remember what I told you," Tanner added. "I'll be in complete control. I won't be a wild animal. I'm just... me. Wade and I will never, ever, hurt you. Our whole focus in on protecting you. Making you happy."

She blew out a breath and nodded. "Okay. Go."

Tanner shifted, and Nancy stared at him, her mouth dropping open. She didn't scream, or shriek, or do any of the things I had thought she might, but she was trembling as if on the verge of a freak out.

I stroked her back, trying to be reassuring, as Tanner sat in his wolf form, then dropped into a simple waiting pose, before finally shifting back to his big human self.

That's when Nancy freaked out. She pushed away my hand, scrambled from the bed, ran into the bathroom, and slammed the door shut. Then she started screaming.

~

*N*ANCY.

I was proud of myself for holding it together. Mostly. I only screamed once before I managed to gulp my panic back down. Then I began to pace, up and down the tiny bathroom. It was only a few steps, but I didn't care. I had to keep moving, shaking my hands and my head and even my feet. "Holy shit! Like, holy shit!"

I couldn't believe what I'd just seen. It was true. They were wolf shifters! I hadn't even known such a thing existed in our world. Did that mean...

The realization that maybe they'd been telling the truth about all of it, began to penetrate the fog of panic. Were they genuinely attracted to me? Was I really their actual... mate?

Was there really such a thing as a perfect pair of men... for me?

I sat down on the toilet, reeking of sex. "Bleh... I so need a shower."

Part of me wasn't exactly hating on the smell, even though it was sweaty and musty, and all kinds of man funky. I stood up, stripped off the shirt that Wade had given me, and stepped toward the shower.

"Nancy?" Tanner called out, his usually laid-back tone a little worried. "You okay?"

"I'm gonna have a shower," I called back, not quite ready to face them again. Wolf shifters! "You guys do whatever you need to do."

"We'll leave you to it then," Wade said in his serious voice. He too, sounded concerned. More than usual.

"I might get Maddi to bring you some more clothes from the shop. Just so you've got something to change into," Tanner added.

Their thoughtfulness got me right in the solar plexus. "You don't have to do that."

"It's no problem. We'll leave you to it."

I turned on the shower and hopped in before I could collapse. My brain was still whirling like a tornado, whipping up every thought and feeling I'd had since I met the boys, analyzing, checking and freaking out.

How had I not known? Were they even human? What the fuck sort of town had I landed myself in?

But slowly, slowly, the water began to relax me, washing away the panic and stress and leaving me strangely calm.

I turned off the water and wrapped myself in a huge towel. I was shivering, despite the warmth of the water, and I craved both Tanner and Wade's warm bodies. The feel of them wrapped around me in bed had been so deliciously soothing. Which was ridiculous. They were... wild creatures that I'd thought only existed in books and movies.

Once I was dry, I wrapped myself in the towel and crept back into Wade's bedroom. The bed was still rumpled, and the smell of sex was heavy enough to make my belly twist with remembered need. Despite finding out that my men turned into huge, wild beasts, the sex we'd shared was freaking amazing.

My men? For fuck's sake.

I was still thinking of them as mine. Even though I knew they weren't human.

I sat down on the bed and groaned. "I'm an idiot. Seriously. What's wrong with me?"

There was a knock, then the door cracked open. "Got you a bag of clothes," Tanner said, his words slightly disjointed as though he was panting from running.

I stood up and shuffled toward the door, holding on tight to my towel that was still wrapped around my body. "Thank you, but you didn't need to do that."

How much money did I owe them now?

"No issue." He placed the bag on the floor and then stepped back, pulling the door closed.

I sighed as I picked up the bag and carried it to the bed. What were the chances that these clothes would fit? Fifty-fifty at best.

I pulled out the clothes that either Tanner or his sister had chosen for me, and couldn't help the smile that spread across my face. Blue jeans, a black top, a white tank, and a red sweater.

"Wow," I whispered as I rubbed the material of the soft sweater between my fingers. I'd never had boutique clothes before. These were beautiful.

At the bottom of the bag was a pack of individually wrapped panties, in my size. "Damn, that girl's good."

No bra though, which I totally understood. Bras were a personal choice, and I was more a sports bra-style girl. No underwire unless I was going out.

My own bra was on the floor near the door, so I grabbed that up, pulled on the new panties and tried on the clothes. The jeans fit like a glove. A little tight around the ass, but all new jeans were. The tops were fantastic, and I put them all on, layering for the cold weather outside.

I walked back to the bathroom to have a quick look and couldn't believe the transformation. What was happening to me? I looked good. Shapely, somehow.

My mind was clear, and the dark clouds were rolling away. I walked back into the bedroom, noting the softness of the carpet beneath my feet. When I opened the door back into the living room, both men were there, sitting on the couch with matching expectant looks on their faces.

They jumped up the moment I stepped into the room.

I swallowed hard, an immediate and massive wave of lust hitting me when I saw them. They'd both pulled on jeans and a shirt. They looked like matching book ends in a way. Opposites in coloring and personality, and yet perfect complements of each other.

"Thank you for the clothes." I felt unaccountably shy, shooting looks at them then quickly away again.

Tanner held out a hand. "You look great."

I didn't take his offered hand, but I did walk closer. "Your sister really does have an eye for this sort of thing."

"Yes," Wade said, his voice deep and husky. "She does. You look..."

I raised my eyebrows. "Nice? Okay? Fat?"

Wade grunted. "I was thinking fucking fuckable... actually."

The compliment wasn't lost on me. They'd just had me, not even an hour ago and he wanted to go me again?

I couldn't help asking, "You think... really?"

Wade marched straight up to me, slid one hand around my waist and lifted the other to my face. I stared up into the darkest, most beautiful eyes in the world for a brief moment before his lips crashed down onto mine.

I didn't fight him or try to pull away. I threw my arms around his waist and sank into the relief that swept through me as he kissed me. There was so much I didn't know about these men, and some of the things I did know scared the shit out of me. But this... this was right. This was true. And the idea of losing the man in my arms, or the one reaching out for me, scared me more than anything else in the world.

And that need, the sense that I couldn't be without either one of these men, no matter who or what they were, was the most terrifying thing of all.

THIRTEEN

When Wade finally pulled away, I didn't run. Instead, I put my head on his chest and cuddled in, letting him soothe me with actions and his presence instead of words.

Tanner came over and joined us soon enough. He took my hand and pulled me into his arms, obviously wanting a hug and kiss of his own. He was taller than Wade and when I snuggled into him, my head fit against his chest, right over his heart.

I could hear its strong and steady beat and the sound filled me with a sense of happiness.

"I'm sorry I scared you," he said into my hair.

I lifted my head and stared up into his eyes. "It wasn't you... exactly. It was more... the whole idea of shifters being an actual, real, thing."

"Come, sit down," Tanner said, guiding me to the couch once more. "Have you got any questions?"

"Um..." I bit my lip, not sure where to start.

"This is weird for you, isn't it?" Tanner asked gently.

I nodded. Yeah, it was. But how did I even start to explain to people who'd been born into this world, just how weird it really was for someone like me.

"What can we do to make you feel better?" Tanner asked.

"We could take her to meet Mom and Dad, maybe?" Wade suggested suddenly.

I managed to smile at that. They wanted to take me home to meet their parents. That was flattering. "Thanks, but I'm not feeling my best at the moment."

"Do you want a tour of town?" Tanner said. "We could go for a walk. Grab some lunch, maybe?"

That sounded nice and I was so appreciative of their care, but strangely enough, all I wanted to do was sleep. Too much had happened, and I felt like my body needed to fully switch off for a short time.

"Could I rest for a bit?"

Wade stood up and held out his hand. "Of course. Come rest in Tanner's bed and we'll go out and do some grocery shopping. Leave you alone to chill for a bit."

"Thank you," I whispered, following Wade into Tanner's bedroom where the bed was still made up and the smell of sex wasn't in the air.

Wade pulled the curtains and Tanner flipped back the covers.

When I sat on the bed, they moved to the door.

"Do you need a cell phone?" Tanner asked suddenly, as if the thought had just occurred to him. "We want you to be able to contact us if you need to. We could pick one up while we're out."

"Thanks," I said, already peeling off my new jeans. "That sounds great."

I was still concerned about the bills racking up, but I needed a way to contact Toni, and Lexie, and my men. So their logic was sound.

"We'll leave you to sleep." Tanner attempted to close the door. But Wade pushed it open again.

"Do you want one of us to stay here? Just so you feel safe?"

Warmth suffused me at his words. They were so caring, in every way. I stripped off my top, not really caring that they might see my lumpy body even in the dim lighting. "I'm okay. You guys won't be long, right?"

Who was going to hurt me here? No-one knew I was here, and normally two big buff men lived here so a random break-in was unlikely.

"Nope. Not long at all," Tanner said, staring at his brother, before pulling the door shut.

I climbed into the queen-sized bed and put my head on the pillow. I liked this room, too, even though it was smaller. It had a great relaxed feel to it, just like Tanner.

My eyes slid closed as my post-orgasm-post-shifter-reveal shock set in. I probably needed to sleep for a week, but I'd start with a few hours. That should be more than enough.

WHEN I WOKE up again the light in the room was different. Bright sunshine was no longer streaming in under the dark curtains. I rolled onto my back and stretched my arms above my head.

God, I felt good. Lethargic and a bit weird, but good.

There were voices talking in the lounge room, but I couldn't make out what they were saying. Probably just Tanner and Wade unpacking groceries.

I pulled myself out of bed, taking a moment to sit on the side of the mattress before hauling up to my feet. "Whoa." I needed a gallon of water and something to eat. I was definitely feeling weird.

When I finally got dressed and opened the bedroom door, I found that Tanner and Wade weren't the only ones in the living room. There was an older man and a woman there too. I hadn't met them before, but they seemed familiar.

"Oh." I stopped awkwardly, not wanting to intrude. "Hello."

The woman stood up and rushed over to me. "Nancy! It's so nice to meet you." She embraced me, holding on tight.

"Ah... it's nice to meet you, too." I instinctively hugged her back, knowing in my gut that she was a good person.

The other man stood with Tanner and Wade. He looked just like Tanner, with blond hair and blue eyes.

When the woman pulled back, I realized she looked just like Wade. She was shorter, darker, and had tears in her eyes.

No prizes for guessing. These two had to be Tanner and Wade's parents.

"They turned up unannounced," Wade said, a touch of anxiety in his voice. "We didn't invite them."

I remembered what I'd said, about not being ready to meet their parents yet. Obviously, he was concerned I'd take offence. I smiled at him, and nodded reassurance. "All good." Then I turned to their mom, who was sniffing a little. "Are you okay?" I asked her, grabbing the box of tissues that was nearby on the table.

She laughed and pulled out a Kleenex, dabbing at her eyes. "Oh yes, I'm just so happy. Part of me had given up hope that my boys would find their mate."

"Oh." I glanced at the guys who were now looking anywhere but at me. "Yeah, I'm still getting used to the idea myself."

"I'm Matilda, Tilly for short," the woman said. "Come, sit. This must be so overwhelming for you."

She waved her hands at the men and they all moved out of the way for her.

I sat next to her, feeling oddly happy to be surrounded by Wade's family. They emanated warmth and happiness. "It is a bit."

How did I explain to them that, for me, nothing had really changed. I was still planning on getting on my Harley and driving to my uncle's place as soon as I could.

Right? That was still the plan?

"You know, I'm human too," Tilly whispered. "Not that anyone likes to talk about it. But the first time I saw my husband shift, I passed out."

I gaped at her. "Really? Oh, that's so good to know." I hadn't thought about the fact that there'd be more women in their family like me.

"Sweetheart, Nancy doesn't want to know about our romance. That was over forty years ago."

I glanced at Tilly's husband, who was sitting perched on the edge of a dining table chair.

"Oh no," I told him. "I want to know. This whole thing has been freaking me out and I want to know how other women cope. It seems like Lexie just took it in her stride."

Tanner walked to the kitchen, brought back a platter of cheeses, crackers and fruit, and set it down on the coffee table in front of us.

I reached for a strawberry, my stomach aching for food.

"Want a drink?" he asked me.

"Water, please," I said, and he left to get me a glass.

Tilly stared after her son. "Yep, raised him right. Anyway, back to the question."

I couldn't help but grin at her. She had raised her boys right. They were honest, respectful, good guys.

"Your daughter Maddi's pretty cool, too."

Tilly rolled her eyes. "Oh, I've given up on that one."

I chuckled at her tone. Mothers and daughters either get along like a house on fire, or bash heads at every interval. It was obvious which category Maddi fit inside.

"Anyway," Tilly said, "I grew up in this town but didn't even realize that wolf shifters existed. At first, I was scared, and kinda freaked out about what that would mean for me, and any babies I had with Frank."

I glanced over at her husband, who was grinning now. When he crossed his arms over his big beefy chest he looked just like Tanner, only older.

"So, how'd you get over it all?" I asked her.

She shrugged. "I wanted Frank. I knew that. So, I just pushed through. I didn't want to be without him. I met the pack, all the women, and they were wonderful. Such a great supportive family, and I wanted to be part of that."

"Is that why you're here?" I asked her, accepting the glass of water from Tanner and taking a big gulp. "To convince me that everything's going to be okay?"

Tilly grinned at me. "Of course, it is. There's no fighting fate, but your life will be a lot easier if you accept it right off."

I wasn't much for accepting my fate. Especially when I felt like I was spiraling into something I knew nothing about.

I patted her hand. "Well, I appreciate the thought. It was really nice of you to come over and meet me."

It was obvious that Tilly didn't care what sort of woman her sons had found, just as long as they had someone. "Do you care that they have only one... wife?" I asked.

Tilly raised her eyebrows at me. "Do you?"

I couldn't help glancing over at my men, who were standing closer to the kitchen, listening. Did I care that if I stayed with them I'd be with two of them? Did I want the one-on-one marriage that Tilly and Frank had?

"I don't know, to be honest," I said, taking the opportunity to talk to a woman who might be able to help me work my way out of the hole I'd found myself in. "I'd never considered it before. I always assumed I would find one guy, maybe, to marry. If I was lucky."

"Maybe?" Tilly repeated, picking up on the one word in that sentence I didn't want her to. "Why would it be maybe? You're gorgeous!"

I glanced away because I knew I wasn't. "That's not true, but it's nice of you to say."

"Beauty is in the eye of the beholder, dear. Most of the girls in the pack think my boys are too old to be handsome now."

"That's bullshit," I said, immediately responding to the slight on my men. "They're gorgeous! How could anyone say otherwise?"

The resounding silence was my answer. No-one had said that, but I'd been fooled into admitting how I felt about her sons.

"Rightly so," Tilly said after a while. "Now, Frank and I should go. But we just wanted to pop in and meet our future daughter-in-law."

I jumped up as they stood, "You can't assume that, surely? I only met Tanner and Wade a few days ago."

Tilly patted me on the arm. "Yes, I know. That doesn't change how they feel about you. Nor how you feel about them, does it?"

Her dark gaze was too probing and I looked away.

"We'll see you boys for Friday night dinner, if not before," Tilly said to her sons, kissing them both on the cheek before she and Frank left.

I ran my hands through my hair and let out a shaky breath.

Wade walked over to me. "I'm sorry. They came by without advance warning, and we were trying to get rid of them when you woke up."

I went up on my toes, wrapped my arms around his neck and hugged him tight. "Don't apologize," I whispered into his neck, the smell of him surrounding me. "Your parents are awesome."

So much more awesome than mine had ever been. My mom had been depressed and had died when I was young. My dad had been a hero to the motorcycle gang, but to me... he'd been absent, and I'd often been put into dangerous situations.

Tanner and Wade's mom and dad obviously loved them and had given them as normal a family life as possible. Friday night dinners, cuddles and affection.

Wade hugged me and Tanner's hand rested on my back. "I'm going to heat up some dinner. Then we can relax and eat."

Tanner disappeared and Wade dragged me to the couch to cuddle. He was good at being quiet, being silent. He didn't try and make me talk, or sort everything out, or even joke around lightheartedly like Tanner often did. He just allowed me to exist. And I needed that.

When Tanner walked in with plates of lasagna and a smile on his face, I took the plate and cutlery and ate, with a great deal of gratitude.

Despite my earlier nap, I was still tired, and when it came time for bed we all climbed into Tanner's bed, and I slept in between the two of them. I had no idea what the future held but I was equal measures of light and heaviness inside, my wariness about getting hurt warring with hope for future happiness.

But with my past chasing me and all my fears and insecurities piling up around these perfect men, I just wasn't sure there was a future for me here.

FOURTEEN

I got up early the next morning and went for a run, in human form. Now that we were home, I wanted to create some healthy habits. Eating real food. Exercising.

When we were on the road, working, Wade and I ate fast food crap. Slept in our truck or hotel rooms and never even shifted. My body felt weak and unhealthy, especially compared to my cousins. Markus and Ollie were pumped and strong. I might be a few years older, but I wanted to be just as capable as they were.

For my mate. For Nancy.

When I got back home, I snuck into the shower, washing away the sweat and dirt. My heart was still pumping hard and my legs shook from the exertion, but I was feeling good. I could get used to living healthy.

Wade was cooking breakfast when I walked into the kitchen, the enticing smell of bacon in the air.

"Morning," I called out, running a hand through my wet hair. "How's our mate. Is she up yet?"

Wade didn't turn, just kept flipping the bacon and stirring the scrambled eggs. "She's still in bed, but she's not asleep."

"And… how is she?"

Wade finally looked up at me. His expression was uncertain. "I'm not sure." Then he went back to cooking, adding tomatoes and spinach to the mix.

The soft padding of footsteps behind me had me turning around to find Nancy standing in one of my shirts in the doorway to the living room.

"I'm okay, Tanner."

"Are you?" I asked, walking forward, but not touching her. "I'm worried about you."

She smiled, then extended her arms out in front of her and twisted her fingers together. "Don't be, I'm happy to be here."

I couldn't help but laugh at her tone. "You sound surprised."

"I'm not actually sure I know how to be happy."

The admission was made with a soft strength.

I pressed my lips together and nodded. "Takes a lot of courage to admit something like that."

She swung her arms like a little kid. "Yeah, well. Lots of firsts for me lately. So, what's on for today? Do you guys have to go to work?"

"No. We're home, so we're not working."

"Food's up," Wade announced, bringing plates to the kitchen table.

I grabbed knives and forks and set the table as Wade buttered toast and served up the bacon and eggs.

"Wow, this all looks so good," Nancy said, staring down at her plate as if shocked Wade had cooked it all.

"Dig in," Wade said, gesturing for her to sit. "I'll just grab drinks."

I sat and encouraged Nancy to do so as well. "Let's eat, and you can tell us a bit about your life. Childhood, pets, whatever."

We all told stories and laughed over breakfast, then Wade and Nancy headed off to get dressed.

"Do you want a tour of the town still?" I asked her when they returned. "Or do you want to go check on your bike?"

Nancy's face lit up. "Oh... Toni's place first, please."

"Done. Let's do it."

We cleaned up quickly and headed out, locking the door on our apartment on the way out.

I took Nancy's hand in mind as we walked toward the main street. "What sort of family house would you like? A new one in town like Lexie and her guys? Or something on a bit more land, maybe? A bit further out?"

I raised my eyebrows at her, but she glanced away.

"What's wrong?" I asked, squeezing her hand.

"I... I don't know how to talk like that."

"You mean like we have a future together?"

Her smile was brief but beautiful. "Yeah."

"Okay, look. You have to understand that, for us, fate has shown us the way. Our future is you. If you want to run to your uncle's house, we'll go with you. If you decide you don't want us, then we'll sleep in our truck in your front yard just to make sure that no-one ever hurts you again."

Nancy stumbled on uneven pavement, and I grabbed her, pulling her against my chest.

She stared up at me, gripping my shirt. "You'd follow me?"

"Not in a stalker way." I grinned at her. "But you have to know that we won't ever date another woman now. If you reject us, you may as well sign us up to the priesthood."

She pushed herself back, out of my arms, out of contact with my skin.

I ached from the loss.

"That's not fair," she whispered. "That makes me feel like I have no choice."

"Oh, you do," I said, smiling as reassuringly as I could. "It's us that don't. Our shifters have chosen you, so we're in. No matter what."

I could see that she was starting to get scared, her bottom lip trembling.

Wade stepped closer. "Can I propose something?" he asked in his usual serious tone.

She turned to him and nodded, as if grateful for the interruption.

"Give us two days to show you what life could be like with us, Nancy. Just two days. If you don't like what we are, who we are, we'll let you leave. And we won't follow."

"Wade!" I hissed at my brother. He knew we couldn't do that.

Wade didn't even look my way. He was focused on our mate.

"Just two days?" she asked.

He nodded. "Yep. But you've gotta play along too. If we ask what sorta house you'd like, you tell us. And if we can't make you happy, if you think we're wrong for you, in two days, we'll wave you off and you and your Barbie Harley can drive off into the sunset."

I looked from Wade to Nancy and back again. I couldn't imagine how much strength it had taken for Wade to say such a thing. He was way more possessive than I was, and my wolf was howling inside my mind at the very thought of letting our mate out of our sight.

Wade didn't mean it, of course. He couldn't. Could he?

"So?" Wade said, pushing Nancy for an answer. "Do you think you could give us the chance to show you what sort of life we could have together? You could stay positive, push away all your fear. All the bullshit. All the past baggage and just... jump?"

Nancy was biting on her bottom lip like a starving woman. It was a lot to ask of anyone. Especially someone who had obviously spent her life fearing the worst and living like tomorrow might not come.

"Okay," she finally whispered.

"Really?" I asked. "You'd do that for us?"

Her eyes began to sparkle a little, rare happiness showing in her face. "Yeah... well, what's the worst thing that could happen?"

I laughed. "That we live happily ever after?"

Wade groaned. "More like... No, I'm not going to say it. Okay, what's the first order of business?"

I reached for Nancy's hand and slid my fingers between hers. "Bike first? Or you wanna talk houses?"

"We can do both, yeah?" she said, then started strolling along the sidewalk once again.

"Sure," I said, keeping pace and grinning at her. "Back to my question. Nice, new house in town? Older one on a property outside of town?"

Nancy glanced back at Wade, trying to include him in the conversation. "Do you need more space, you know, to run?"

I chuckled. "We don't need it, but more space after living in hotel rooms and trucks for a decade would be nice."

"Yeah," Wade agreed. "Though just being near the forest's edge would be enough. It's what most of our cousins do."

Nancy hadn't answered, so I squeezed her hand. "What's your preference?"

She shrugged. "I've never had a real home so I wouldn't care if it was a trailer home on your parents' property, as long as we owned it and no-one could take it away from us."

My heart squeezed tight in my chest. Damn. She'd lived harder than I'd realized. "I think we can do better than that."

"Definitely," Wade said, grabbing Nancy's other hand. "My turn. Come with me."

I let go of our mate and trailed behind my brother as he dragged her down Main Street all the way to the real estate agent. He stopped in front of the shop.

I stepped up behind them and Wade said, "We don't like to talk money and crap, but our place is paid off and we've been saving for a while."

That was an understatement.

"And we can go out and buy you any one of these." Wade gestured to every house in the window. "Today."

"This one is ridiculously big and needs a shit ton of work, but it's on ten acres out of town." Wade pointed to another one. "This is down the road from Lexie's place. Super new, not big but..."

Nancy turned around and launched herself into Wade's arms, hugging him tight.

"You okay?" Wade asked, gently stroking her back.

She pulled out of his embrace and nodded, wiping the tears from her cheeks. "You're actually serious, aren't you?"

"I'm always serious, haven't you worked that out yet?"

I had to chuckle at that. "Considering Wade's the serious side of the perfect pair, he is definitely bloody serious."

Nancy covered her eyes with her hands and half-sobbed, half-laughed before dropping her arms once more. "Okay, well in two days' time, if I'm staying, let's come back and choose one."

I liked the sound of that.

Wade gripped her shoulder and twisted her back around. "But for fun, choose one now."

His gaze slid over to mine and I had the sinking suspicion that Wade was about to spend a whole lot of money on a home, before the forty-eight hours were up.

He had always been one for grand gestures.

Nancy leaned forward and peered into the window. "I kinda like that one." She pointed to a historical home that needed work.

She went on. "It's probably tired on the inside too, but it still looks like a home. Lexie's house is nice but there's no real soul to it."

I slung my arm over her shoulders and peered at the listing. "One point five acres about two minutes' drive from Mom and Dad's place. Looks like a good one. Great taste, sweetheart."

She smiled up at me and Wade stepped forward to peer at the listing she'd chosen. "We can check it out tomorrow."

"Seriously?" She sounded shocked.

I laughed and lowered my head so that I could kiss her sweet lips. "Yes, seriously. We've got two days to spoil you and show you what life will be like with us. One thing you should know is that we work hard and make decisions quickly. If we all like that place, we'll get it."

She frowned at me. "You mean it'll go on a short list, right? You can't buy the first house you see."

I cleared my throat and agreed with her. "Yeah, of course. We'd look at others, too."

But that wasn't what I meant and even if I didn't make a move on that property, I was pretty sure Wade would. It would take an act of God to stop us buying something that could make Nancy happy. If she chose to stay.

She said she'd never had a true home before. We'd make her one, or build her one, or buy her one. Whatever would make her heart sing. Because the only priority we had now was keeping the mate who'd stumbled onto our path and changed our lives forever.

FIFTEEN

NANCY.

My bike was on the mend, and I was in two minds about that fact. Because once it was done, and paid for, there would be no reason not to continue to my uncle's place. Leaving Tanner and Wade behind. But on the other hand, it was wonderful to see my beautiful bike looking so good.

"Toni, I can't thank you enough for this." I ran my hand over my beautiful baby.

Toni wiped her hands on a dirty rag, then smudged oil over her sweaty forehead as she brushed back her hair. "I've got a few things to tune before you can ride it again, but give me two days, and you'll be good to go."

Wade made a strange sound and I rushed over to Lexie. "I brought my card to pay today, though you haven't let me know what the invoice total is."

"Oh well, since you're sorta part of the pack now, the parts are at cost price and you can pay for the labor whenever you can."

My mouth dropped. "I'm not... you can't..."

Lexie whipped my card out of my hand and walked back into the office. "I'll put the parts through."

I stared back over my shoulder at my guys. "But..."

Tanner stepped up and slung an arm over my shoulders. "Sweetheart. Don't stress. We told you. Money's nothing to us. We can cover the lot if you want?"

I shook my head avidly. I couldn't cope with all this generosity. I wasn't used to it. "No. Please. I..." Tears burned my eyes and I gulped in a breath and held it. I didn't want to cry. Not now. Not when everything was going well.

Lexie came back into the room and handed me back my card. "I know what it feels like to have no money and to grow up feeling like you owe everyone; that you have to scrape by. What you'll find here is that money is not important. The pack looks after it's own, so just say thank you. And shut up."

Lexie grinned to soften her words and I managed to swallow down my tears and nod. "Okay."

"Let's go for a walk," Wade said, heading over toward the exit. "It's still light."

I nodded, still struggling to get all my emotions in order. "Okay." Then I smiled again at Toni. "Thank you so much."

"Any time," Toni said with a shrug. "You know I could probably use another worker around here, if you end up sticking around."

"Really?" I asked, sliding my gaze over to Lexie, who was standing by the office doorway.

Toni crossed her arms. "Yeah. Lexie doesn't work every day and if I know wolves, which I do, she'll be pregnant soon enough."

"Hey!" Lexie protested, but I could see happiness light up her eyes at the thought.

Toni's eyebrows fluttered up. "Just sayin'. I could use another helper, that's all."

I took Tanner's hand as he tugged me over to where Wade stood waiting. "If I stay in town, Toni, I'd be grateful for a job, thank you."

"No problem," Toni called out, waved at me, then went back to working on my bike.

When I stepped out into the sunshine I felt as if a weight had lifted from my chest. I still felt fragile and emotional and over-whelmed. But my mind was clearer and my heart sang with unaccustomed happiness.

"Where do you want to walk to?" I asked the boys.

Wade studied me and then smiled, as if he could sense my inner joy. "Anywhere is fine by me. Let's do a lap of the main part of town, then grab some takeout from the diner on the way home."

That's exactly what we did. The guys walked me around the town, pointing out shops and schools and houses where their family lived, and I enjoyed listening to the pride in their tones as they spoke.

When we finally got back to their apartment with our dinner, I was exhausted and ready for a night on the couch. We watched a movie and fell asleep early. I couldn't imagine being anywhere else right now, nor could I ever imagine being happier than in this moment. As I was drifting off to sleep, I made the decision to call my uncle in the morning and let him know that I wasn't coming to live with him now. That I'd visit him, and soon, but that I'd found a place, and people, to call my own.

AFTER ANOTHER COOKED breakfast made by the guys, Wade headed off to make a few clandestine phone calls and then hurried me into the truck.

"Where are we going?" I asked, laughing at the obvious enthusiasm of the guys.

"You'll see," Wade said, hopping in the driver's seat.

I hadn't yet called my uncle but I had time. I hadn't changed my mind, especially not after the way the guys had made love to me this morning. Slowly, beautifully, but with so much need and passion that I sobbed as I came. Again, and again. I had never felt like that about anyone before. Let alone two guys at once.

"Okay." I grinned at him, reaching for his thigh and placing my hand possessively on him. I'd never thought I could be a woman who could be in a relationship with two men, but being with Wade and Tanner was as easy as breathing.

"Is Tanner coming?" I asked glancing back and realizing he hadn't followed us.

"Yeah, he's just getting the other car out of the garage."

The sound of a heavy, revving engine met my ears and then an old, black muscle car rolled toward us.

"Whoa," I said, enjoying a rush of pleasure at seeing such a hot car. "That's... wow. Why don't you guys drive that one all the time?"

Wade pulled the truck out onto the road and Tanner followed us. "This is the work car. That's the home and relaxing car. It hasn't been driven much, to be honest."

I chuckled. "You guys work too much?"

Wade snorted. "That's an understatement."

"How come?" I asked, enjoying having Wade alone for a moment. Tanner was the talker and often Wade hung back, quiet and serious as he watched Tanner take the conversational lead.

He glanced over as we slowed to a stop at a red light. "We didn't have a reason not to work. When we hit thirty, it became obvious that our fated mate didn't live here in town, so we got a job that meant we traveled a lot."

"You were looking for the one?" I asked, feeling strange in my stomach. They'd been looking for me, all that time.

"Yeah." He spoke softly. "We've been insanely lonely for... well, a long time. So we just worked. And worked some more. There was no reason to stop."

I waited a heartbeat before asking, "And now?"

He grinned at me, actually grinned and his serious face lit up. I sucked in a breath at his beauty. "Now that we've found you, I'll happily never work on the road again."

He pressed his foot harder on the gas pedal and turned the car off the main road and into a suburban street with older-style houses on large, private blocks. I didn't ask any more questions until Wade pulled up in front of a house with a "for sale" sign out the front.

I pressed my hand to the cold glass window. "Is this the house I pointed to yesterday?"

"Yep," Wade said simply. "Let's go check it out."

He opened the door and hopped out. I followed him. Yeah, it was the house I'd pointed to. The block was huge, and the house was gorgeous, even though it was obviously in need of some sprucing up. Covered with winding vines, a terraced roof and beautifully detailed, stained-glass windows.

"It's beautiful," I breathed, looking past the surface to the bones underneath.

Wade chuckled. "Ah... this place is gonna take a year just to underpin and clean up the block. And that's not taking into account any work required on the inside."

He didn't seem put off, though. He grabbed my hand and tugged me toward the gate. I hesitated, wanting to wait for Tanner so the three of us could look at it together.

A white sedan pulled up behind Wade's truck and a woman jumped out. She had curly red hair and a big smile. She was beautiful, and thin, but there was something about her that I just didn't like, despite that smile.

"Wade!" She bounced toward him like a gazelle. "So good to see you again."

She went up on her toes and tried to kiss him. He turned his cheek just in time and I gaped at them.

"Um... I'm sorry. Who are you?" She had to be the real estate agent, but it was obvious she was a lot more to my man.

She turned to face me, her gaze immediately scanning me from head to toe. Clearly, she didn't like what she saw. She made that obvious with an unsubtle grimace.

"I'm Kellie," she said. "And you are?"

"Our fated mate," Tanner announced, walking up to stand beside me.

I lifted my chin and smiled at her. I might not yet be one hundred percent sure that I wanted the fated mate title or that role, but I wasn't telling this bitch that.

Kellie's eyebrows rose high on her forehead, so I reached for Tanner and Wade's hands, gripping their fingers tight. "Yes. And these two want to buy us a family home, so go open the door and do your job. Please." I wasn't sure why I needed to stake my claim so clearly, but I couldn't bear the thought of this woman getting her hands on either one of my men.

She narrowed her eyes for a moment before plastering on another fake smile. "Of course!"

Then she pulled a tangle of keys out of her bag. "We have a lot of houses on our list that are in better shape than this one. I can show you those afterward if you have time today."

I glared at the back of her head as we followed her, marching up the path to the house. "I like this one. Thanks."

Her spine stiffened as she slid the key into the hole. "Well, you haven't seen the inside yet."

I glanced up at my men. "What do you two think?"

"We think that if you like it…" Wade said.

"Then we'll strip it to the studs and rebuild it if we need to," Tanner finished.

It was the first time I'd seen them do the twin thing and finished each other's sentence, and from the look on Kellie's face when she turned around, she hadn't seen them do it either.

"Let's look then," I said, letting my men's hands go. I pushed past the bitchy real estate agent and stepped into a grand foyer, dominated by a large winding staircase. My heart beat fast and my breath hitched in my throat. For the first time in my life, I was home.

SIXTEEN

WADE.

The sound of a motorbike convoy rolled through town as we finished up looking at the house. Even though we were away from the main part of town, the noisy revving of engines filled the air like smoke.

Tanner took our mate back to our place, because she was dying for a ride in the 'hot car', as she called it. I went back to the real estate agency with Kellie who wasn't doing much to hide her envy. She had been an occasional bed mate of mine, and I knew Tanner's, too, but there'd been no real meaning or affection behind our occasional catch-ups.

She seemed more put out now that I wasn't giving her attention, than any genuine sadness that our catch-up days were clearly over for good.

"Put in a full price asking offer," I instructed, sitting on the chair opposite Kellie and her computer. "Let the owners know we'll pay cash. And the place is obvious empty, but also confirm we want to be in within the week."

Kellie's jaw dropped, then she tried to recover by turning to her computer screen. "The owners moved out about a year ago, so it might take me a few hours to track them down and get a response."

I stood up and dusted off my jeans. "Well, the cash, full price offer is only for the short settlement date, Kellie. See what you can do."

I turned and made it to the door before she called out. "How can you be happy that she's your mate?"

I stopped and faced her. The vitriol that dripped in her tone when she referenced Nancy showed her true nature. Kellie was a mistake of the past, nothing more.

"How can I not be happy?" I crossed my arms over my chest and stared at her. "She's perfect for Tanner and me. Fate chose her for us, and I can quite honestly say I've never been happier in my life."

Kellie's blue eyes were vicious. "She's fat. And ugly. And human."

My hands tightened into fists. "If you were a man, Kellie, I'd knock you into next week for those words."

She leaned forward over the desk and glared at me. "You could have married me, or anyone from the pack. Who the hell do you think—"

"Enough!" I roared. "Tell the pack. Tell the women. Tell everyone in the state. Tanner and I are off the market. Nancy is our mate and if any of you hurt her, by words or physically, then God help you."

I threw open the door so hard it banged against the wall. Kellie yelped, and I stormed out. "Bloody bitch."

I knew she'd do her job, for the commission. The wolves weren't altogether money focused, but some shifters did like the finer things, including Kellie. And the finer things cost money. That was one of the main reasons Kellie and women like her had wanted us. Tanner and I had more money than most, and we didn't spend it, which made us even more desirable.

When I burst through the front door the fresh air hit my lungs and I inhaled fast. As the anger dissipated, I exhaled more slowly, and relief soared into my system. We were going to buy a house, a proper house. A home.

We'd have our mate and life would finally be complete. We'd waited long enough.

My truck was parked out the front of the real estate office, but I wanted to walk. Tanner would no doubt be keeping Nancy busy and if he was like me, alone with our mate, he'd be taking her back to bed for another session.

I enjoyed thoughts of her happiness, and hoped she'd be up for another round when I got home.

I stopped by the diner to pick up some wraps and chicken schnitzels for lunch, then wandered down our street. I was almost at our building when the scent of blood met my nostrils. What the hell? I hastened my steps toward home. The roar of a motorbike revving up almost drowned out a woman's terrified scream.

Nancy? "Oh, hell no." I dumped the food on the sidewalk and took off running.

A huge Harley took off just as I got to our building, Nancy on the back, clinging to the rider, her face red and screwed up like she was crying. She looked back at me, her terrified eyes clearly begging for help.

"Nancy!" I chased after them, but the guy drove faster down the road away from me.

My wolf jumped to the forefront, and it was only the mostly human neighbors, outside their homes gaping, that stopped me shifting.

I stopped running. "Tanner. Where the hell's Tanner?" My brother wouldn't just let some asshole on a bike take our mate away without a fight.

I turned and raced back to our building, the grass at the entrance dug up from the spun wheels of multiple bikes, and the front door hanging off its hinges.

"No," I whispered, stumbling in to our apartment to find that door also broken. I almost tripped over pieces of furniture that had been tossed everywhere. My brother was lying face down in a puddle of blood. And he wasn't moving.

I fell to my knees beside him and used all my strength to haul him over onto his back. "Tanner!" I yelled, pressed my palm to his chest. There was a heartbeat.

But barely. I checked his body for any wounds I could help to heal. His face was a mess, with a broken nose, two already-swelling eyes and a cut on the side of his head.

None of that should have had him unconscious.

I lifted his shirt and there it was. A bullet wound in his upper chest. "Son of a bitch." They'd missed his heart by inches.

I pressed my hand to the wound to slow the flow of blood, tears filling my eyes as I grappled for my cell phone with my free hand.

I hit 911 and called paramedics. The town had a small hospital, thankfully, and I was certain they'd be here soon, especially when I explained to the operator that Tanner had been shot in the chest.

Next I called my parents. "Mom. Dad. I need you to meet Tanner at the hospital. He won't be long, I'm guessing. Ten minutes. Tops."

Mom's gasp was loud. "What happened?"

My blood was running ice cold through my veins, but my mind was clear. Whoever had done this to Nancy and Tanner, would die.

"Bikers came. Took Nancy. Shot Tanner. I was..." I gulped, trying not to let guilt swamp me. "At the real estate office. Buying a house."

"Is he alive?" she whispered, a question no mother should ever have to ask.

"Yes." I swallowed back the urge to add, for now, and took a deep breath. I had to stay calm. The sirens were getting close. "I have to go deal with the ambulance."

I put my hand on Tanner's chest, which was still rising and falling.

"Wade?" Dad's voice was urgent in my ear. "How can we help?"

"I need the pack, Dad. We have to find Nancy, and that man who took her." I didn't want more of my wolf shifter family to get hurt, but Nancy was everything to my brother and me. I couldn't stand by while a man stole her from us.

"Your mom will go to the hospital. I'll meet you at the old church, okay?"

I nodded, even though he couldn't see me. "Thanks, Dad."

I hung up as the paramedics came in and dropped down on the carpet with me. They assessed his wounds and bandaged up what they could. He also had a knife wound in his side that I'd missed, and his face was a mess.

"We better get him to the hospital," Amber said. She was a girl I'd gone to school with. A human, but she knew about shifters, and I knew he'd be in safe hands with her.

"You riding in the ambulance, Wade, or wanna follow in your car?"

I stood up and watched as they loaded my huge, barely alive brother onto the gurney. They placed an oxygen mask over his face, and he groaned, his arm swinging around.

I grabbed for him, not wanting him to hurt anyone. "Tanner, it's me. It's Wade. You're okay."

I stepped up and stared down into his panicked eyes. "Nan... cy."

"Yeah. They got her. But don't worry, Dad and I are on it."

"Wade."

"Tanner." I gripped his hand tightly. "I'll get her back. Go. Heal. I won't give up. I promise."

Tanner let go of my hand and closed his eyes.

I looked at Amber, "The guys who did this took our partner, Nancy. She..." I gulped, "I have to get her back. Our mom will meet you at the hospital."

Amber nodded once, concern in her expression. "Good luck."

I grabbed my keys, ran outside and jumped in the sports car, and took off. The abandoned church Dad had referenced was on pack lands in the forest. Secluded, but not too far away.

As soon as I arrived, I jumped out of the car and started to strip. My wolf was hungry for the hunt, and the smell of those motorbikes, and blood, was still in the air.

My dad's truck pulled up, full of family. Then Uncle Mark's crew and Toni on her bike. People piled out of cars and trucks.

Markus and Ollie pulled up, jumping out with Lexie on her bike not far behind them.

"What happened?" Toni asked, already stripping out of her leathers.

I was down to just a pair of jeans. "Long story short. Nancy, our mate for those of you who don't know—"

"We all know," Uncle Mark cut in. "We were giving you time with her. Go on."

"Nancy grew up in a motorcycle gang and her dad died. She got in deep with a bad guy there and was running away from him when her bike broke down. I don't know how they found her, but they did. Tanner's alive, but they beat him to hell, stabbed him and shot him in the chest. Then they took Nancy away."

A deep, angry rumble rolled through the group.

"These guys aren't messing around. They're packing and they're dangerous." I glanced at Markus. "I'm not sure Lexie should come. She's human."

The racking of a shot gun sounded in the air. "And I'm one of the only people in this pack who can handle a gun."

"Me too," Toni said, pulling out her own shot gun. "Lexi will ride with me. The rest of you shift and run. We'll follow."

Dad grunted. "I'll drive too. In case they get past the valley, and you need a break from running."

I hadn't thought about that. But Dad had. I could always count on my family. "Yeah, thanks."

Dad nodded and headed to his truck.

My gaze fell on Lexie. "If something happens to you..."

Lexie opened her motorcycle jacket to show me a strange vest she was wearing. "I've got Kevlar. My over-protective mates got me covered. Don't worry. I'm not leaving Nancy. Never."

Tears tingled in the back of my nose and throat, but I didn't let them fall. "They have about fifteen minutes head start. Let's go."

I let my wolf take over. My skin turned to fur. My heart beat faster. Dirt beneath my paws and my nose was filled with smells I couldn't distinguish as a human.

The church yard filled with growls and snarls and the sound of Lexi and Toni revving their motorbike engines.

I turned and took off, following the scent of the motor bikes who'd taken my mate. The roads around our town are windy and long, but we could run through the forest. Cut them off. Trap them in the valley before they hit the highway.

Or die trying.

I could barely breathe. Blood and snot ran from my nose, and tears covered my face. I didn't want to hold onto Travis, but I'd fall off the back of the bike if I didn't, and he was traveling fast. So, I clung to his jacket with the tips of my fingers and leaned away as much as I could.

Travis was riding like a bat out of hell, three of his guys following behind us. They were all damaged, bleeding and injured. Thanks to Tanner. He'd fought like a fury to stop them from taking me.

I gulped as fresh clogged up my nose and throat. Tanner. Oh my God, they'd shot him. Please let him be alive.

Tanner had been holding me, kissing me, when Travis had kicked in the door and entered with several of his mates. Tanner had fought so bravely, and he'd keen kicking their asses when Travis had pulled out a gun and shot him. Shot Tanner. My beautiful, big, gentle giant.

He'd gone down and one of the other guys had then pulled out a knife and stabbed him, as if being shot wasn't enough. I had thrown myself over him at that point to try and stop them. I'd gotten a kick and a punch too, and from the pain in my back and side, I probably had a broken rib. I didn't care.

I wanted to go home. I wanted Tanner. I wanted Wade. And I prayed that these guys, carrying me back to the club I'd grown up in, would die and go to Hell. Quite literally.

They might be Hell's Angels, but I was praying to whoever was listening that some demons, not angels, would come and drag them away.

I yelped and grabbed hold of Travis harder as we rounded a curve in the road. I didn't remember the road coming into the town as being this bad.

I glanced around. This wasn't the road I'd come in on. Where were they taking me?

I closed my eyes and tried to figure out what to do. I wasn't wearing leathers, or a helmet for that matter. I couldn't afford the risk of jumping off and hoping I'd survive.

No-one was coming for me. I would have to deal with this on my own. Somehow.

Once we stopped, I could fight. But with what? I didn't have my knife, and I didn't own a gun. How was I going to fight for my life against armed and very dangerous men?

And what did they want? Me? Back in the club? Or buried in the cemetery?

I didn't know, and for a strange, chilling reason, I didn't really care. If they'd killed Tanner, I'd die. Literally. Even though I still wasn't sure about the whole wolf shifter thing, I knew one thing. Those men were mine. We were meant to be. Everything in my heart and soul told me it was true. We were linked, body and spirit.

And I had no idea how I would live a life without them.

I'd always believed I didn't deserve what other people had. Love. Marriage. Babies.

A happy-ever-after.

But I'd been so close to achieving that impossible dream. My men had loved me. Accepted me. Been ready to buy us a home and offer me a future. In fact, they'd been so grateful to find me, it had terrified me at first.

What sort of men talked like they did? None I knew. And their intensity had been shocking. But so wonderful I'd had moments where I'd believed I must be crazy, or dreaming.

And I had be, to think even for a moment that I could get away from my past, or that it would stop hunting me.

Finally, the bike began to slow, and Travis pulled over in the middle of nowhere. There were fields, surrounded by forest. No houses or people that I could see. My stomach fell and gripped with ice. "Where are we?"

"Piss stop." He swung his leg off the bike so violently he kicked me off and into the dirt.

I landed with a yelp, scratching my hands on the gravel.

"Take a moment, boys." He waved a hand at his men and then sauntered off to piss behind a tree.

I staggered up to my feet and wiped my face with my sleeve. Thank God I had a sweater on. A bloody expensive one, but still. It had protected my skin a little, from the gravel.

"You're gonna pay for this, you bitch."

The viciousness in Travis's friend Harry's voice had me turning around to face him.

"For what?" I whispered. "I didn't do anything."

I was only half-prepared for the smack when his hand struck me across the cheekbone. I gasped in pain, deliberately falling sideways to the ground so he didn't do it again. I needed my strength for later. For my final stand.

"You ran!" He yelled down at me, standing over the top of me. "You stupid, fat, fuck. Travis had your father's mantle. His drug runs. Everything. But you had to stay. You fucked it up, and you're gonna pay now."

I had no idea what he was talking about. I'd never been a part of any of those side of things in the club.

Travis strolled back to the bike, buckling his belt. "Yeah, well boys. Don't worry. She'll pay. I was thinking we might tie her to the whore's bed and let the club guys have at her."

I grimaced and looked away. I'd die first.

"The guys don't want her," one of the other guys scoffed. "She's fat."

"Let her starve for a few weeks," Travis said. "That'll trim her down."

I didn't say anything as he grabbed me by the front of my sweater and hauled me to my feet. I kept my head down and my gaze on my feet, in case Travis saw the glint of determination in my eyes.

I wasn't giving up. Not now. And if they got me back to the club, I'd shoot myself before they had the pleasure of seeing me tied up and on display for the club's men.

A lot of the guys were still loyal to my father. One of them might do me the mercy if I asked.

Travis got back on his bike and even if I'd had a faint thought of running, Harry crowded me until I had no choice but to slide on behind Travis. My body was sore, but adrenaline was pumping through me, pushing aside the pain so that I could still think.

"What the hell is that?" Travis said, looking around and then up at the sky as though he was expecting to see a storm.

I frowned and lifted my head, listening. That wasn't thunder, or a storm. That was the growl of a wild animal. More than one. A thundering sound added to the growl and a shot of exhilaration raced through me.

Wolves growling and motorbikes approaching? Wade was coming for me.

I wasn't alone in this fight.

"Trav!" One of the guys called out. "Can you hear that?"

A huge gray wolf leapt from the cover of the trees and Travis gunned the accelerator so hard he stalled the bike.

"Jeezus!" he yelled.

The wolf came hurtling toward us and I scrabbled to get off the back of the bike.

"Stay there!" Travis screamed at me, panic and fear in his voice.

I ignored him and jumped off the bike, running toward the wolf.

No, make that wolves. I'd been right. There had been more than one growl.

In fact, it looked like there was a whole pack of them. Gray and black and brown. All huge, and terrifying.

But not to me.

I fell to my knees and the gray wolf bounded up, leapt over the top of me, then landed behind me.

I rolled over onto my ass to stare at the wolf who was snarling at the bikers but wasn't budging. He was protecting me.

Travis spat curses in my direction, trying to force me up and back to him. But I wasn't going back and he wasn't getting to me through the beautiful big wolf that I had to assume was Wade.

The other wolves drew close, all snarling and growling and eyeing the other guys. With shouts of fear, most of them took off on their bikes. Travis reached for his gun and I started to scream, swallowing the sound back down when the wolves charged at him. I saw the moment he changed his mind and decided to forget shooting and drive off instead. I would have done, too, if I had a whole pack of huge snarling wolves running at me.

He re-started the engine and took off down the road.

Two bikes and a truck came roaring down the road from the direction of town, and I managed to get to my feet just as the bikes pulled up. Toni popped her helmet up.

"You okay?" she called out.

I nodded and stumbled toward her. My heart was racing like my life was on the line, which it had been.

"Go, Wade," Toni called out.

I turned to stare at the wolf who had protected me. "Thank you," I whispered, and the wolf nodded.

The truck drove past and pulled over. Wade and Tanner's dad poked his head out of the window. "Hop on the tray!" he called out, but Wade was still not moving, and I realized it was because of me.

"Go," I said, letting my love and appreciation show in my eyes. "Go get him. I'll be okay."

I wasn't okay. I didn't want him to go, and possibly get hurt, or worse. I wanted Wade to stay with me and be safe. But I knew what those guys had done to Tanner. And my beautiful blond mate needed to be avenged.

Lexie walked over, pulling off her helmet. "We've got her, Wade. We'll take her back to the hospital to be with Tanner. You go catch that asshole."

"Wait!" I ran to the wolf and dropped to my knees, sinking my face into his luxurious fur. "Be safe, my beautiful shifter." I pulled back and managed to smile at the wolf, who nuzzled my cheek before he turned and leapt on to the back of the truck.

The truck took off and hot tears welled and slid down my cheeks. Lexie pulled me up, spun me around, and hugged me tight.

"You okay?" she whispered into my ear.

I pulled back, nodding, even though I wasn't. "How's Tanner?"

"He's alive," she said, handing me a spare helmet. "Hop on."

I pulled the helmet over my crazy, wind-whipped hair, and got on the back of Lexie's huge bike. I tried to focus on getting back to town, to Tanner. But it was almost impossible not to think about Wade, racing after my ex, possibly to further injury.

I couldn't lose either one of them, and my heart hurt to think about what could be happening to Wade right now.

EIGHTEEN

WADE.

I was still shaking from seeing Nancy beaten and bruised, her eyes red-rimmed and her face tear-stained. I hadn't wanted to leave her, but I trusted Lexie to get her to Tanner, and I needed to hunt down Travis and make him pay for what he did to my brother.

I'm going to kill him. Travis is dead.

Dad took off after the bikes, driving the truck like a bat out of hell. The road was tough to navigate around here, but Dad didn't slow down. I crouched low in the back, trying not to get thrown out of the tray.

He slammed on the brakes as we took the next corner and the sound of my wolf pack snarling and growling reached my ears. I was thrown forward and rolled, hitting the back of the cab.

I leaped to my feet and jumped off the back of the tray. My uncle and cousins had taken down two of the men and pulled them off their bikes. They were ripping into the guys, biting their hands and jumping on their leather-clad bodies.

Travis had gotten away. Slimy bastard. He was on foot though, as his bike lay on its side in the dirt. I scanned the terrain and saw movement on a rocky outcrop. Travis was climbing, aiming to get to higher ground. He had a gun, and from up there he could possibly pick us all off one by one.

I wasn't letting him use that gun on my family.

I charged past Ollie and Markus who had hold of another biker and leaped up onto the rocks close behind Travis. He turned faster than I expected for such a big man and raised the fun, firing. I ducked, the bullet whizzing over my head.

I growled and launched at Travis, snapping my jaw and baring my teeth in his face, pushing both paws against his huge chest. He over balanced and fell, landing hard on the ground. Unfortunately, I toppled with him but managed to roll and get to my feet once more. My cousins Ollie and Markus must have finished with their guy, because they charged and got hold of Travis's arms with their teeth, stopping him from picking up the gun that had landed a foot from his right hand.

He punched at them like an old boxer, vicious and fast, trying to throw them off. He was fighting for his life and he knew it, so he wasn't as scared as he should be.

One of his punches landed and Ollie got knocked to the ground with a yelp.

I saw red.

And I needed to face him, man to man. I made a decision that could be fatal, and I knew it. But I wasn't letting these guys get away with kidnapping my mate and almost killing my brother. They had to pay.

I shifted back to human and stood tall, staring down at the man who'd taken my mate from my home.

He froze, stopping his fight with the other two wolves.

Ollie and Markus backed away, kicking the gun further out of Travis's reach, and then stared between us.

Travis staggered to his feet.

"What the hell are you?" He breathed heavily behind his helmet.

"Take that fucking thing off," I growled. I was also breathing hard, and my chest was rising and falling too fast. I had to get control of my body. I was still shaking from the adrenaline and shifting too many times when I was out of practice.

Travis hesitated, then reached for his helmet and pulled it off. He had a half-decent face, and part of me recoiled in jealousy that this man had been with Nancy.

"What the hell are you?" he repeated, glancing behind me.

I checked quickly, to find that the other guys were being held down by my pack members, and Dad was standing by the truck, a shot gun slung in a seemingly casual manner over his arm.

I turned back to Travis. "If you get in the truck nice and peaceful, we'll drive you to the nearest police station and I won't beat the hell out of you like you did my brother."

Travis sneered. "That guy Nancy was shacked up with was your brother?" He spat on the ground. "I hope he's dead."

My hands tightened into fists and my wolf rose up, hard. I pushed him down just as fast. The only way I wanted to hurt this asshole was with my fists. I'd use my claws and teeth if I had to, but I wanted him to know exactly who he was dealing with.

I said through clenched teeth, "If he was dead, I wouldn't be standing here talking to you."

"Then what are you waiting for?" Travis lifted his arms to gesture offensively. "A personal invitation? Faggot."

I charged at him, ducking his punch to pop up and swing at his head. I connected and pain exploded through my hand and arm. He took the hit and countered with a punch to my gut.

I groaned and staggered back. Fuck, this guy packed a punch, and I was out of practice. I brought up images of Nancy's stricken expression as he'd hauled her off, and Tanner's broken body, to inflame my anger. I attacked again, punching him as hard as I could in the body before delivering an upper cut to his jaw.

He blocked me and weaved out of the way, then he attacked. He kicked my knee, and I heard a crack as one of my legs was taken out from under me. I went down, rolling out of the way of his stomping boot as he tried to break my nose. Fucker.

Then he reached for his pant leg, tugging it up and pulling out a huge knife.

Oh fuck. I got to my feet and jumped back as he swung the knife at my belly. He was trying to kill me.

The wolves were howling behind me, ready to jump in if I needed them.

I ducked his next punch, then his knife caught my ribs, slicing through my flesh. I pressed my hand to the wound, blood seeping through my fingers.

Fuck. I was going to die. All because I was out of practice at fighting. I wanted my brother. I wanted my mate. I fell to my knees, my head spinning as blood gushed down toward my thigh.

Travis advanced, coming in for another blow. He lifted his arm above his head, the silver knife glinting in the sunshine. This was it. I'd failed my family. My pack. My beautiful mate.

A shot gun blast sounded behind me, the shot hitting Travis square in the chest. I turned my head slowly. Behind me my dad stood there like an old western hero, shot gun smoking as he lowered the barrel. He stared at the man who'd almost killed both of his sons with a hatred I hadn't known existed in my dad's heart.

He went back to the truck, pulled a length of rope out of the cabin, then threw the rope at my cousins. "Tie those guys up and throw them in the truck. Leave this bastard here to bleed out. We'll send the cops out after we get back to town."

Travis was still alive, groaning and gurgling, his hands scrabbling against the wound in his gut. "Call an ambulance," I said to Dad. "If we leave him here... you can't go down for murder, Dad."

He came over and offered me a hand. "I wouldn't, not in this town. That was self-defense. Pure and simple."

I grabbed his hand and dragged myself to my feet, pressing my hand against my side. "Call them, Dad."

Travis deserved to die and part of me knew that if we dug a

shallow grave and tossed him in it, no-one would blame us. In fact, the pack would back us up. But we had two other witnesses who were protesting being tied up.

"Dad," I repeated, understanding that my father would voluntarily go to jail if he had to save my life and avenging my brother, but I couldn't live with that. "Please."

"Fine." He pulled out his cell phone and called the paramedics and then the police.

When he hung up, he turned to me and my cousins. "You all need to shift and get back to town. Especially you, son. You'll heal much faster in wolf form."

He was right, of course. I just wasn't sure I had the strength for yet another shift so soon.

Markus walked up to me. "Come on cousin. It's gonna hurt, but no worse than the hospital would put you through while stitching that up."

I nodded and took a deep breath. He was right, of course. "You okay with them?" I asked my father.

My uncle Jack shifted back and walked over to the truck, reaching in and pulling out a spare set of clothes. "I'll stay too, Wade. You go. Get back to town and your mate. And if these fuckwits say anything about us, I'll kill them myself."

There was a gasp and then a pained groan from the bikers hogtied in the tray of the truck, and I smiled at my uncle in thanks.

I limped toward the forest and took a couple of shallow breaths before asking my wolf to jump up and into my injured body again. It hurt like fucking fire, but once the transition was complete, the bleeding in my side slowed and my shifter genetics kicked in to begin the healing process.

I began running, slowly at first and then faster, following my cousins back to my mate and my brother.

NINETEEN

TANNER.

When I emerged into consciousness, the ugly beeping of hospital machines hit me straight away. People were talking, murmuring nearby, and I had something plastic shoved up my nose.

I couldn't seem to open my eyes. They felt like they were glued shut. But I reached up anyway, groaning and tugging at the plastic tubes in my nose.

"Tanner! You're awake."

That was Nancy's beautiful voice, and I was so filled with a startled happiness, I sat up and managed to force my eyes open. "Oh my God, beautiful. You're here."

How had she gotten free of those guys?

"You're gonna rip your stitches open," she said, pushing me down with a gentle touch. "Lie back."

I grabbed her arms and hauled her closer to kiss her. Pain filled my belly, but I ignored it and held her against me. The injuries would heal. The moment I realized my mate had returned somehow from a biker kidnapping would not happen ever again.

She chuckled against my lips and didn't fight me as I kissed her, then she reached for the bed controls and sat me up.

"Thanks," I said, feeling more comfortable as she put a pillow behind my head.

Wade wandered into the room, then, a big smile widening his mouth despite a whole bunch of bruises decorating his face.

"What the fuck happened to you?" I asked, wincing as I shifted too sharply amidst the ugly white hospital sheets. "I wanna go home. When can I go home?"

I glanced over at my mate. "How long have I been out?"

Wade pulled up a second hospital chair next to the bed, sat down, and Nancy slid back down into the chair closest to the bed. I reached for her hand and she gripped my fingers, holding on tight.

She started talking first. "Okay, well, you've been unconscious two days."

"Fu... what?" A shifter wasn't unconscious that long unless he was dead. I glanced at my brother. "She being serious?"

Wade reached over and patted my thigh once, then nodded. "Yeah. Those fuckers shot you, stabbed you, and beat you unconscious, brother. You're lucky to be alive."

"We're lucky you're alive," Nancy added.

"I need to say something." Wade coughed, uncomfortable now. "I should have been with you. Both of you. This wouldn't have happened if we'd been together."

"Oh no, don't say that." Nancy grabbed Wade's hand with her free hand. "If you'd been there, things could have gone so much worse. You both could have been shot. Or worse. I couldn't bear the thought of losing either one of you. But both of you?" She shuddered, and my fingers tightened reflexively around hers.

I frowned at Wade. He couldn't take the blame for this. I had the feeling that I was only sitting here alive because of him. "How am I alive?"

Wade pressed his lips together. "I found you, called the ambulance, then went after Nancy. With the pack."

I managed to laugh, even though my throat was sore and dry. "Man, you saved my life. And you got our mate back. But what happened to your face?"

Wade shrugged. "I played a part. But so did all the others. And it was Dad who really saved the day." He gave us a rundown that ended with our father shooting Travis in the gut.

"Fucking good," I snorted. "Hope he gets thrown in jail and they toss away the key."

Wade and Nancy looked at each other, then back at me.

I frowned. "What did I miss?"

Nancy slid a little closer. "They brought Travis in to this hospital and patched him up."

I growled and shifted in the uncomfortable bed. "Hope he's suffering."

Nancy grimaced as though I'd said something awkward. "Actually... he's dead."

"What? How?" Had Dad come back to finish the job? Had Wade?

Wade actually grinned. "Idiot broke out of his hospital room, attacked the guards and got shot by Gary."

Gary was the Chief of Police.

"Whoa," I said, gaping at them. "So... he's gone?"

I could barely believe it. The guy who'd shot me and kidnapped our mate was dead?

"Yep."

"Dad's not getting in trouble?" I asked.

"No, not at all," Nancy said with a smile.

I lifted Nancy's hand and kissed her fingers. "So you're not riding off into the sunset anymore? Or did we fail the forty-eight-hour test?"

Nancy stood up and leaned down to kiss my lips. "Oh, I'm never leaving you guys. Never, as long as you want me."

"Want you?" I laughed, tugging her down for another kiss. "We need you in our lives. Forever."

Wade stood up suddenly and handed Nancy a set of keys.

She lifted them up, looked at the silver keys attached to a simple key ring, then jangled them. "What are these for?"

I grinned at my brother, not needing Wade's explanation to know what they were for. "I knew you were going to do that."

Wade, like me, had enough money to buy that house without me putting in.

"I put it equally in all our names," he said, though he was still staring at Nancy. I was going to let him say it. I wasn't stealing his thunder. He'd had the balls to go ahead and buy a house for our mate. For us. For our future.

"Wade?" She prompted him, obviously still confused judging by her tone.

"They're the keys to our house," he said simply. "The one you liked."

Her jaw dropped. "The fixer-upper on that huge block?"

I laughed. "You mean the one you almost cried in because you thought all the features were so beautiful?"

Nancy stared from me, to Wade, then back again. "Is he kidding?"

"Nope," I said, shaking my head to accentuate the point. "And I'm assuming my brother offered cash, so the house is probably settled, with no mortgage."

Wade glanced down at the ground, embarrassed. "Yeah... well. Seemed like the right move."

"Wait." Her hand fluttered at her chest. "You said before... you said... you put it in all our names?"

Wade's cheeks pinked up and I grinned at him. "Yeah," he said. "It's for all of us, after all. If... if you want it, that is?"

Nancy flew at him, throwing her arms wide and hugging him tight. She began to sob, but she was also laughing. Then she turned and hugged me, too.

When she was finally calm again, she wiped her face with the Kleenex by the bed and sat down. "I can't believe you did this for me. For us. What if I'd decided I was going to my uncle's and not coming back? Oh shit... I need to call him."

Wade smiled. "We wouldn't have given up on you."

She laughed. "Not sure I want to know."

I laughed too, tugging her up on the bed so I could kiss her again. "Wade. Go find out when I can go home with you guys."

Wade left us alone and I kissed my beautiful mate and told her how much I adored her.

When my brother returned, he brought Tommy with him. A doctor, and a member of our pack.

"Hey Tommy," I said, reaching out to shake his hand. "You part of the team that fixed me up?"

Tommy was a few years younger than us. He shook my hand and grinned at me. "Of course. Someone has to try and hide the advanced healing you took on. Everyone else would have died if they'd seen you come back from a knife wound and bullet to the chest within two days."

I frowned at him. "Thanks for that, but I'm not impressed it took me two days to wake up. That's fucked."

Tommy chuckled. "Thank your brother for that. You were bleeding out. We were lucky we got to you when we did. Coz super healing or not, you wouldn't have come back from that."

I looked over at my brother. "Told you. You did save my life."

Wade grimaced in a slightly embarrassed way and went back to talking to Tommy. "Can he come home?"

Tommy glanced at the beeping machines. "Stats look good. Can you guys give me five minutes to check him out, then I'll give you a professional opinion?"

Professional or not, I was going home.

Wade and Nancy indulged Tommy and went looking for a coffee machine.

Tommy peeled off my dressings, inspected my wounds, then re-dressed them.

"You know I'm going home tonight," I told him. "Right?"

Tommy sighed. "Of course, I do. Your stubborn ass is famous."

I grinned at him. "Great."

"Your mate is lovely." He spoke quietly, a longing in his voice. Tommy was one half of a perfect pair, too. He and his brother David had never married or met their fated mate.

"She is," I said proudly. "Had to wait freaking decades for her, but it was worth it."

Tommy went to the end of the bed and made some notes in my chart. "Yeah, I can see that." He sounded sad.

Then he lifted his head and was back in professional mode. "You can be discharged, but you'll need to come back tomorrow, just so we can check those stitches and change the dressings. You're still nowhere near healed, Tanner. And take some of the good pain meds for tonight."

I nodded, willing to agree with anything he said just to go home. "No probs, Doc. Do you know where my clothes are?"

He chuckled. "Yeah, I think your brother threw some in that closet there. I'll give you a few minutes to change, and I'll go be creative on your discharge forms, so I can let you go home."

"Well," I said, as I carefully swung my legs over the edge of the bed. "If you'd set up your own clinic, us wolves wouldn't have to come to this hospital, and you wouldn't have to 'be creative'."

Tommy rolled his eyes. "Yeah right. I'd go broke waiting for patients. We get one, maybe two pack members in here a year."

I got to my feet, a little light headed but feeling great considering. He was right, of course. We didn't often get sick, and our advanced healing meant that unless we were dying, literally, there was no reason to consult a doctor.

"Thanks Tommy."

He nodded and left, shutting the door behind him.

I stretched slowly, my body achingly sore. But I was alive. And Nancy had agreed to stay. That was all that mattered.

I pulled out the clothes Wade had left for me and slowly got dressed. It was time to go home and heal. After all, I had years of house renovations ahead of me.

CHAPTER

TWENTY

NANCY.

It took Tanner three days of cuddles, sleep and food to recover to the point that his sutures could be taken out and his scars began to disappear.

I was up a ladder, washing down a wall in what was going to be our dining room, when Wade came in. "How are you going, beautiful?"

"Good," I said, grinning down at him. "I love this house so much. What did Frank say?"

Frank was the electrician and apparently knew everyone in town.

Wade shook his head. "You don't want to know. Tanner's on his phone looking up vacation spots for next week."

I frowned at him. "Huh? How is bad news about the house leading to a vacation?"

Shouldn't there be cursing and checking bank balances and working out what we were going to do?

Wade shrugged. "Frank said the whole house has to be re-wired, but the good news is, the foundations are good."

Fuck, re-wiring would be expensive.

"What about the plumbing?" I asked. We hadn't moved in here

132

yet. We were still living at the apartment and just coming here during the day to renovate, but I already loved this place so much I couldn't wait to move in.

"It's not too bad," he hedged. "But Frank's going to bring in a friend tomorrow and assess properly."

That didn't sound good, either.

I grabbed the bucket and climbed down the ladder, brushing the hair out of my sweaty face. "I still don't get what that has to do with a vacation?"

Tanner ambled into the room with a big grin on his face. "Frank told us to clear out for a few weeks. He's gonna bring his team in and get all the structural work done before we do anything else."

I waited because there had to be a point. "Yeah? And? We have an apartment we can stay in until then."

Tanner grinned. "Yeah, but Wade and I haven't had a vacation in over five years, and since we can't work on the house for a few weeks, why not go to Hawaii, or Vegas, or even Canada? You got a preference?"

A vacation? A real one? "Oh... I've always dreamed of visiting Hawaii."

"Hawaii it is then," Wade said.

"Cocktails on the beach would be amazing," I said, before worry hit me hard. "But money..."

"Isn't an issue," Tanner said, cupping my face and kissing me lightly. "We've been working and saving for the time we finally had our mate. Let's go enjoy it."

I hugged him tight and thanked the universe again for the gift of my men.

We headed home to the apartment, had dinner and I was having a long hot shower when Tanner wandered in, naked and beautiful.

I grinned at him through the glass panel. "You coming in?"

He quirked an eyebrow at me. "We were hoping you'd finished your shower."

Oh. "Are you sure you're okay? Your shoulder..."

"Is healed. As is the rest of me. But there's one part that is really in need of some TLC."

A quiver of excitement shot through my belly as my gaze lowered to the part in question. He was so sexy, but I'd tried hard not to think about that while he healed.

Quickly, I turned off the shower and grabbed a towel. We hadn't had sex since before the 'incident.' I'd missed them, but I'd waited. They'd both been hurt, not just Tanner, and up to now, sleeping with them every night had been intimate enough to keep my heart happy.

But my body craved more. So much more. Need pooled between my legs. "All right, I'd love to."

I dried myself quickly, watching Tanner's cock get harder and longer before my very eyes.

"Great, let's go." He took my hand, his tone impatient enough to make me giggle.

They'd set up the room while I was in the shower. The soft lamps on either side of the huge bed were lit. The bed covers were dragged back and Wade was also naked and very clearly waiting for me.

I couldn't help but smile as his cock hardened the moment I walked into the room. It was titillating having not one but two men who proudly showed their unmistakable desire for me with such enthusiasm. "What? No candles and seductive music?" I teased.

Wade walked toward me. "Do you want candles? And seductive music?"

I shook my head. "No. I just want you."

I turned to Tanner. "And you."

Tanner let go of my hand and I went into Wade's arms, lifting my face to enjoy his kiss. He wasn't gentle. His impatient touch added to my need as he grabbed me and hauled me against his body, pushing the towel out of the way and dropping it to the ground.

I kissed him back, thrusting my tongue into his mouth to taste him. God, I'd missed him. I'd missed them both.

When Wade finally lifted his head he said, "You never truly told us what you felt after that first time we were together. Did you feel the connection? Do you feel the fated mate bond like we do?"

I glanced over at Tanner, then back to Wade. They were waiting for an answer. I had assumed that my actions spoke enough for how I felt, but it seemed that they needed the words, too.

"I did feel it then," I said, gulping as nerves assailed me. Words of affection didn't come easily to me. I hadn't had much of that in my life. Until now. "But the feelings I have for both of you have only increased since then. When Travis and the guys came to take me back to my old life, I'd never been so afraid. Not just for what they would have done to me in the club, but to be leaving you. I would have rather died than not seen you two again. I felt like my very soul was being ripped apart.

There were several moments of silence before the strange tension dissipated. Tanner grinned. "Yep, sounds like our mate link is strong and in place, but there's one way to make it even stronger."

I sniffed and tried not to let more tears—even if they would be happy ones—taint the beautiful moment we were all sharing. "Yes? What's that?"

"A wedding for one," Wade said, his smile filling my heart with utter joy.

"And more sex," Tanner added, always the one to lighten things up. "Of course."

Now there was no holding back the tears. "You want to marry me?"

Tanner chuckled. "Of course, we do. We love you, with all of our hearts and souls."

Wade cleared his throat. "Both of us. Hearts and souls, Nancy."

Tanner added, "We can have a mating ceremony with the pack whenever you want, and if you want the human-style white wedding, we can do that too, though legally you can only marry one of us."

I didn't like the sound of having to choose between them. I'd ask Lexie what she had done and go from there. I swallowed hard and managed to say, "A mating ceremony with your family and pack in attendance would be… perfect."

"They're your family and pack too, now," Tanner said, taking my hand and drawing me against his naked body. His cock was still hard and pressing against my belly, making my insides ache.

"True," I managed, though my voice was breathless at the feel of his erection heating my skin. I lifted up on my toes to kiss Tanner's lips. "I love you."

I turned my head to look at Wade, who was watching me with a smile. "You too. I love both of you, Tanner and Wade. So much."

I hadn't said it before, and although my stomach fluttered with nerves, it felt so right to utter the words out loud.

Tanner swung me up in his arms and carried me to bed. "Now it's time to mate with you properly. Prove to you repeatedly that we're meant to be."

He placed me on the bed, and I moved quickly, swinging around to lay on my belly, my head at the end of the bed. I hoped they never stopped showing me how much we were meant to be, and if that meant more of the mind-blowing sex we'd already experienced, then that was truly brilliant.

I stared up at Tanner, wetting my lip with the tip of my tongue.

He stared down at me as though he wasn't certain what I was offering. I didn't want any more uncertainty. "Come here, Tanner," I said. "I want to suck you."

I was so confident in my beautiful men's need for me, I didn't even worry about how my ass might look in this position, or what they'd think of me for being clear about the desire I felt for them. Their love had given me confidence in myself as a beautiful woman, and I wanted to give back to them as much as they'd given me.

Tanner stepped closer and I opened my mouth to receive his cock. God, he tasted good. Hot and salty and beautiful. I moved on him, moaning as my body responded to him with a hot rush of wetness on my thighs.

He rocked his hips and moaned, and his cock thickened, before he pulled away.

I swallowed the saliva in my mouth and looked around for Wade. He was watching me with lust turning his eyes shiny. "You too, please."

Wade stepped up, my serious beautiful man with the tiny smile lifting his lips. I took his cock in my hand as well as my mouth, and sucked on the head, exploring the ridges with my tongue.

When he pulled back it was with a growl.

"Now it's your turn to be pleasured," Wade said.

Tanner crawled on to the bed and lay on his back. "Nancy, come grab the headboard and sit on my face."

Oh my God, that sounded so naughty. And so damn enticing, I couldn't resist.

I crawled up the bed and, without worrying about any of my normal insecurities, I threw my leg over his head and grabbed onto the headboard.

He grabbed my ass with both hands and hauled me closer, eating my pussy like a starving man. Sensation rushed through me and I ground against him. "Oh my God!" I gasped as he licked up and down my seam and flicked my clit, suckling my flesh until I was writhing and bucking against his mouth.

Somehow, along the way, Wade had climbed onto the bed too, and gotten close enough that his hands grabbed and kneaded my breasts, before lowering to brush feather-light strokes across my writhing belly and back up again to flick my nipples.

When I couldn't take any more, Wade seemed to know instinctively and his hands dropped away. I fell back onto Tanner's chest, panting with the need to come. Tanner's expression was wild, his need obviously as great as mine.

"Can we take you together?" he asked, his voice hoarse. "Wade would need your ass."

Fear skittled through me but I pushed it away. These men would never hurt me. "Yes. How do we do that?"

These were my mates, the men I was going to marry. The men fate designed me for. Surely my body could handle them both.

Tanner wriggled down the bed, taking me with him. "Climb on my cock and then lean forward and kiss me."

We were right down the end of the bed now, and when I glanced at Wade he was stroking his cock, watching me with intent eyes.

I did what Tanner urged me to do, climbing over his lap before moving up to position the head of his cock at my pussy entrance.

He grabbed my hips and thrust up into me, making me cry out at the incredible sensation. He thrust again and again, then settled, making my head spin.

"Sorry," he growled out. "But your pussy is so wet and ready I just had to."

I was on the edge of coming, my clit throbbing. "Please. Hurry."

"Come here, beautiful," Tanner said, gripping my arms and dragging me down to kiss him.

His lips were sweet, and I slipped my tongue into his mouth to taste more of him.

Wade's hands were on my ass, rubbing cold lube over my hole and pressing his thumb inside me. It burned a little, but in a strange way, I was aching there too. I wanted both of them now with a level of need I'd never felt before.

Tanner kept kissing me, thrusting his hips gently and making my pussy spark and clench.

When Wade removed his thumb, I gasped out at how empty I felt.

I pushed back against him.

"Ready?" he asked.

I moaned loudly. "Oh yes. Please."

He pressed his cock to my ass, and I pushed against him. The head slid in easily.

I rocked with him, taking an inch of him at a time, feeling so full I was bursting. But I couldn't get enough. It felt so damn right it was insane.

"Oh damn," Wade groaned, holding perfectly still.

My eyes squeezed tight. "Please fuck me," I whispered, not sure which of them I was speaking to. Both. I wanted both to move. "I need to cum."

Wade pulled back and thrust into me again while Tanner gripped my hips and fucked up into me.

My breath caught in my throat, my orgasm building on the edge of pain.

"Oh fuck. Baby. You've gotta cum." Wade gripped me hard, plunging deep inside me.

When he came, the pulse of his heat was the final push I needed. My legs tightened and my belly shook as I was cast off the cliff and into infinity.

"Oh.... Fuuucck." Tanner thrust into me hard and fast, his orgasm heating me at my core and making my orgasm last longer and longer.

Lights flashed behind my closed eyelids and waves of heat rolled over me. Over my back and down my legs, centering deep in my belly where my men were.

Wade pulled out of me and collapsed onto the bed beside me.

Tanner cried out, calling on my body for a final orgasm, wringing the last of the pleasure from my body.

When I finally rolled off him and fell onto the bed, my body was still convulsing with the aftermath of the most amazing orgasms of my life.

Wade and Tanner cuddled around me before pulling up the blankets and kissing my hair, my back, my lips.

"So," Tanner said, still panting a little. "What do you think? Fated, or not?"

I stared up into his clear blue eyes and managed a breathless laugh. "Definitely fated. I love you."

I kissed him hard, then turned and kissed Wade. "I love you," I told the other half of my perfect pair.

"Love you," Wade returned, nuzzling into my neck as Tanner repeated the words in my hair.

I closed my eyes and silently thanked God, Mother Earth and the universe for stopping my bike in this town and making me see that my future held so much more than I'd ever thought possible.

EPILOGUE

NANCY.

Twelve months later

I gulped down the acid rising in my throat. Bloody morning sickness.

Tanner walked into the newly renovated country-style kitchen and gave me a pitying look. "Hey sweetheart. You want me to get you some breakfast?"

I shook my head and sipped my peppermint tea. "No thank you. This is fine."

He rubbed my back, and I tried not to whack him away. I appreciated his care, but I was fine.

My stomach rolled and I gulped down another swallow of tea. Okay, so maybe I wasn't feeling great. But I wasn't the first woman to be pregnant, and I certainly wouldn't be the last.

I managed to get to my feet, kiss him good morning, then tipped my tea into a travel mug.

"You heading out?" he asked, putting on the coffee machine. It was Saturday morning, and our house was finally finished. We were having a huge housewarming party this afternoon and were going to announce my pregnancy.

Ten weeks along and healthy as a horse. Allegedly. I felt like shit. But apparently, that was a good thing.

"I'm just going into town to pick up a few more party supplies, then it's set-up time. I'm so glad your sister and mom are helping so much."

Tanner leaned against the counter. "Mom suspects, of course, but we haven't confirmed."

I sighed. "Yeah. She keeps looking at me strangely, too."

"You sure you don't want me to come with you?"

"Nah, you've got outside to set up. I won't be long."

The boys had finished the pergola yesterday and were putting out all the furniture and setting up the fire pit. All the cousins were coming by to help out soon.

"I won't be long." I walked outside and jumped in the new car the boys had bought for me. It was huge, but safe and would be great when the baby arrived.

I drove the few minutes into town, picked up the cake, the platters and a few select bottles of non-alcoholic bubbles for me and Lexie.

Lexie had given birth to her baby a few months ago and was breastfeeding, so she wasn't drinking, either.

I was walking out of the party shop with a stack of paper plates I'd special-ordered, when a woman walked toward me.

She was beautiful, but I'd never seen her before. The town was small, and the boys had made sure I'd practically met everyone my age.

"Hey," I said with a smile, then noticed her large pregnant belly. "Are you okay?"

She gripped her belly and staggered a little. I grabbed her arm and helped her to the bench seat only a few steps away. "Sit. You poor thing. What's going on?"

The woman shook back her long, light brown hair, panted, and leaned forward. "I'm sorry. You were going somewhere."

"I'll just throw these in the car. Don't stress. I'll be right back." I hurried to the car, threw the plates into the back seat and grabbed a bottle of water from my stash in the trunk.

"Here," I said, opening the fresh bottle and handing it to her. "I'm Nancy. I don't think we've met."

She took the water and gulped it. "I'm not from around here. I'm Stacey."

"Stacey." I smiled. "Me either. My bike broke down while I was driving through town and I never left."

She drank some more water then smiled up at me. "Thank you for that."

She didn't give me any more information, and I needed to get home. I had a party to host and I was starving. But every time I glanced at the car, I felt the strangest urge to help the pregnant woman sitting on the seat in front of me.

"Hey, can I give you a lift somewhere? Or call someone for you? Something?"

She had a backpack but nothing else on her. "Thanks, I ah... I'm looking for someone actually. A man."

I grinned at her. "Well lucky for you, I know a lot of the guys in town."

She gave me a funny look and I burst out laughing. "Oh, not like that, my partners... err, partner, has lots of cousins in town. I can probably point you in the right direction."

She wet her lips, moaning a little as she got to her feet.

"How far along are you?" I asked.

She wore a pair of black leggings and a tight, long black top. But there was no hiding the basketball-shaped bulge.

"Um... about six months, I think."

She thinks? Hmm... this was getting curiouser and curiouser. As was the urge to help her. "So, who are you looking for?"

"Um… his name is Tommy. He's tall," she said, gesturing to a size that matched Wade. "Around six foot two, maybe. And blond-ish."

"Yeah, I know Tommy." And his perfect pair brother, David. Maybe the urge to stay and help this woman was more than just the usual concern for another person?

I grinned at her. "How do you know him?"

She paled, gripping her belly. "Well…"

My jaw dropped. No way. "Is Tommy the father? Does he know?" The doctor I knew would never have abandoned a woman carrying his child.

And what was David, Tommy's twin, gonna say to Tommy getting a woman pregnant without him being involved in some way? Did that even happen, for perfect pairs? I was still learning about the whole perfect pair phenomenon.

"Oh… ah…"

This chick looked exhausted and confused. "How did you get here?"

"The bus," she said, grabbing up her backpack and clutching it.

Oh crap. She's running away from something. Or running to Tommy. Either way, I didn't like the feel of what was going on here and I wasn't about to leave her here alone.

"Come on, Stacey. I've got a housewarming party to put on, and you're coming home with me."

She shook her head. "Oh, I can't inconvenience you like that."

I grabbed her elbow and gently started towing her toward the car. "Tommy will be at the party this afternoon. No idea where he is now, but I know where he'll be in a few hours. So come, shower, eat. I promise, you're safe with me."

She stared at my face for a few long seconds, then let me corral her into the car.

"This is nice." She touched the dashboard.

"Yeah, it's new. I'm pregnant too, but only ten weeks, so no-one really knows yet."

"Oh, congratulations." She smiled brightly at me. "Your husband must be happy."

I laughed. "Yeah. Let's get home and you can meet them."

"Them?" She repeated the word with a squeak, and I didn't bother answering. I just pulled the car out of the parking spot and headed home. She'd find out the truth soon enough.

~

THE END... until book 6!
Pre-order the final Perfect Pairs book:
https://books2read.com/shifterbabe